Another

Episode S/O

novel by
yukito ayatsuji

manga by
hiRo kiyohara

YEN ON

NEW YORK

Another Episode S
CONTENTS

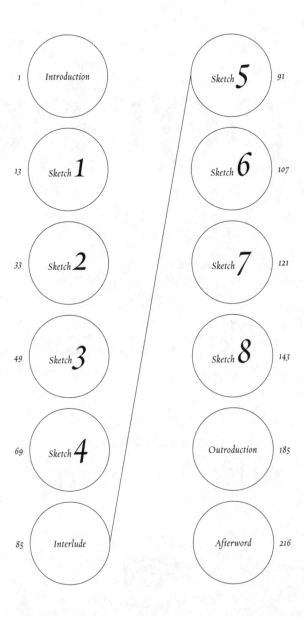

Another 0
CONTENTS

The pages of the *Another 0* manga have been presented in their original right-to-left reading order. The story begins at the back of the book, on page 280.

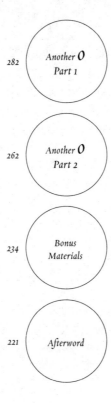

Another Episode S
Yukito Ayatsuji

Translation by Karen McGillicuddy

© Yukito AYATSUJI 2013

Illustration by Shiho ENTA. Edited by KADOKAWA SHOTEN. First published in Japan in 2013 by KADOKAWA CORPORATION, Tokyo.

English translation rights arranged with KADOKAWA CORPORATION, Tokyo, through TUTTLE-MORI AGENCY, INC., Tokyo

Another O
Original Story: Yukito Ayatsuji
Manga: Hiro Kiyohara

Translation by Karen McGillicuddy

Lettering by Katie Blakeslee, Lys Blakeslee

© Yukito AYATSUJI 2012

© Hiro KIYOHARA 2012

Edited by KADOKAWA SHOTEN. First published in Japan in 2012 by KADOKAWA CORPORATION, Tokyo.

English translation rights arranged with KADOKAWA CORPORATION, Tokyo, through TUTTLE-MORI AGENCY, INC., Tokyo

English translation © 2016 Hachette Book Group, Inc.

Yen On
Hachette Book Group
1290 Avenue of the Americas
New York, NY 10104
www.hachettebookgroup.com
www.yenpress.com

Yen On is an imprint of Hachette Book Group, Inc.
The Yen On name and logo are trademarks of Hachette Book Group, Inc.

The publisher is not responsible for websites (or their content) that are not owned by the publisher.

First Yen On edition: May 2016

Library of Congress Cataloging-in-Publication Data

Names: Ayatsuji, Yukito, 1960– author. | McGillicuddy, Karen, translator. | Kiyohara, 1981– Another O.
Title: Another Episode S / O / Yukito Ayatsuji ; translation by Karen McGillicuddy.
Description: First Yen On edition. | New York, NY : Yen On, 2016. | Series: Another ; 2 |
Identifiers: LCCN 2015048928 | ISBN 9780316312318 (hardback)
Subjects: LCSH: Horror fiction, Japanese. | BISAC: FICTION / Horror. | COMICS & GRAPHIC NOVELS / Manga / Horror.
Classification: LCC PL8675.Y38 A8613 2016 | DDC 895.63/6—dc23 LC record available at https://lccn.loc.gov/2015048928

10 9 8 7 6 5 4 3 2 1

RRD-C

Printed in the United States of America

Another

Episode S

yukito ayatsuji

~To Dear A.K.~

Introduction

I

"Would you like me to tell you about it?"

Mei Misaki's voice broke the silence. Her willowy fingertip stroked—slowly—down the white cloth of the patch covering her left eye.

"Would you like me to tell you, Sakakibara? A story from this summer that you don't know about?"

My response was to cock my head. "Huh?"

"A story that you don't know about from this summer. About another person called Sakaki. That interest you?"

In the twilight haze that was typical of the doll gallery "Blue Eyes Empty to All, in the Twilight of Yomi" of the town of Misaki, Mei's smile looked a little strained. She seemed to be hesitating, too—and more than a little—even though she was the one who'd brought it up.

"I'll tell you the story, if you promise not to tell anyone else."

"There's another person called Sakaki...?"

"Not Sakakibara, though. This person's name is Teruya Sakaki."

She showed me the characters that formed the name. Teruya Sakaki. I'd never heard of the guy before.

"You remember how I was away from Yomiyama for a week before the class trip in August?"

"Oh…yeah. You and your family went to your vacation house at the beach, right?"

"That's when I met him."

"This Teruya Sakaki guy?"

"More like, **I met his ghost.**"

"Say again?" My head tilted to one side again. "His ghost…? So, you mean, like…"

"Mr. Sakaki passed away this spring. He died. So when I saw him this summer, it was his ghost."

"Er, do you think…?"

"It's not related to the phenomenon in Yomiyama. Nothing on the level of the casualty in third-year Class 3." Mei slowly closed her right eye, then opened it again and said, "No, he was definitely a ghost."

She knew because the "doll's eye" hidden below her eye patch had the power to see the color of death. That's how she **knew…**

A dubious feeling took hold of me, and I darted my eyes from side to side as I breathed in the chill, stagnant air in the display room there in the basement of the Twilight of Yomi.

The phenomenon for this year came to an end the night of the class trip in August, then summer break concluded and the second semester started…It was the end of September, with the season fading steadily toward autumn. I remember it was the afternoon of the fourth Saturday of the month, a day off from school. I had gone to Yumigaoka Municipal Hospital to get the prognosis on the lung surgery I'd had after the class trip, and I was on my way back home.

On a whim, I had decided to visit **this place**, after so long away.

As it happened, the gallery on the first floor was closed. I hesitated over whether to buzz on the intercom to the Misaki family residence on the top floor, but in the end I decided not to and was starting to walk away when I got a call on the cell phone I had stashed in my jacket pocket—

It was from Mei Misaki.

"Sakakibara? You are outside my house, aren't you?"

I was startled—how could she have known that?—but she blandly replied, "Just a guess. I just happened to be looking outside..."

"From the third floor? Totally by chance?"

I hastily craned my neck to look up at the building. I could see a wisp of shadow move at one of the windows on the third floor.

"Are you calling from a cell phone?"

"Yeah. I had your phone number written down."

Mei had told me that she'd thrown her cell phone into the river right after the class trip. But she'd also told me that Kirika had still made her get a new one as soon as she found out...

"Looks like the gallery is closed today, huh?"

"Grandma Amane has actually been sick, for a change."

"Huh."

"You want to come in?"

"Oh...um, could I?"

"It has been a while since you've come to visit. Kirika—...My mom went out today and everything. I'll come down and let you in. Be right there."

2

I think it's been two months.

If my memory's not mistaken, the last time I'd been to the gallery was July 27. That day, which was also the anniversary of the day my mother passed away fifteen years ago so soon after giving birth to me, Teshigawara had asked me to come to the café Inoya. I'd come here after that.

That must have been when Mei told me that she and her family had gone to their vacation house.

"My father's back."

Mei's expression had seemed to darken ever so slightly with those words.

"He wants to go to our vacation house with my mother. I'm really not thrilled about it, but this happens every time, so I can't exactly say no."

"Where's your vacation house?"

"By the beach. It takes about three hours to get there by car."

"Outside Yomiyama?"

Well, yeah. There's no beach in Yomiyama, is there?…

I'd been waiting a lot longer than Mei's promised "be right there" when she arrived to wave me into the deserted interior of "Blue Eyes Empty to All, in the Twilight of Yomi."

With the clatter of a chime over the door, Mei Misaki appeared wearing a black, long-sleeved dress sparsely dotted with blue stitches. Her left eye was covered by an eye patch, as always.

With nothing more than a "come in," she headed toward the staircase in the back leading to the basement.

As I followed behind her, I noticed Mei was holding a sketch-book under her arm. It was octavo sized, with a dull olive cover.

The sight of the crypt-like gallery in the basement, with its innumerable dolls and doll parts arranged in every available space, hadn't changed in the slightest from when I'd been there two months ago. The only additions were a table and chairs set in a corner of the room: a small round table painted black and two chairs with armrests and red upholstery.

"Go ahead," Mei said again, inviting me to sit. "Or would you rather not talk here?"

"No, it's fine." I sat in one of the chairs, then put a hand to my chest and took a breath. "I think I'm used to it now."

"You're on your way home from the hospital, huh?"

"How could you tell?"

"You told me the other day."

"Oh. I did?"

I appreciated her remembering. My prognosis had been extremely good. The lead physician had also given me the welcome news that since I'd gone ahead and had the surgery, the risk of a re-re-reoccurrence was extremely small.

Mei sat down in the chair on the other side of the round table and set the sketchbook she'd been carrying down on the table. I looked at the drab olive cover. A "1997" written in tiny numbers in one corner caught my eye, and I murmured, "I thought so."

"Thought what?"

"That's not the sketchbook you usually carry. The cover is a different color. Your usual one has a tan cover. Plus this one has 1997 written on it."

"You're a lot more observant than most people."

"Does that mean it's your sketchbook from last year? Why are you carrying it around?"

She must have brought it down on purpose.

"I thought I'd show it to you, Sakakibara," Mei replied with a hint of a smile.

I asked, "Is there some extra-special picture in there?"

"I wouldn't go that far." Mei let out a short breath, then straightened her posture and raised her eyes. "But I do think it might be kind of meaningful."

Kind of meaningful? For what?

"Okay, well..."

I'd started to speak, but I couldn't think what to say next and sat under Mei's unwavering gaze, at a loss, until she spoke.

"Would you like me to tell you about it?"

Her willowy fingertip stroked—slowly—down the white cloth of the eye patch covering her left eye.

"Would you like me to tell you, Sakakibara? A story from this summer that you don't know about?"

3

Teruya Sakaki—the other Sakaki.

Mei told me that she'd first met him the year before last, in the summer of 1996. Mei was thirteen at the time. Her first summer break as a middle school student, taken as usual at her family's vacation house.

"The family of one of my father's acquaintances lives near there—not that far from our vacation house in Hinami. The acquaintance's name is Hiratsuka, and we visit each other's houses and sometimes have get-togethers, kind of like dinner parties…"

I wonder who does the cooking when the Misakis are hosting? The inconsequential thought flitted through my mind.

I doubted Kirika was any good at cooking, and Mei's abilities were close to zero. So her dad, then?

It didn't matter at all, but Mei seemed to have read my mind.

"He's the one who does it…my father on the Misaki side. He seems to like it, I guess since he's lived overseas so long. But the food is mostly catered, stuff like that…"

Oh. That sounds plausible.

"And then the summer before last, Mr. Sakaki came with that other family. He was Mr. Hiratsuka's wife's little brother."

Mei reached out to the sketchbook on the table, flipped the cover back, and picked up a photograph tucked inside.

"This was taken then," she said, gingerly handing it to me. I made some noises of solemn acknowledgment, "Hmm, yes," and dropped my gaze to the photo. It was a five-by-seven-inch color photograph.

It looked like the terrace of the vacation house.

It showed Kirika and Mei, standing there looking bizarrely unchanged despite the fact that the photo had been taken two years ago (though she wasn't wearing an eye patch)...and there were five other men and women in the picture.

"Where's your eye patch? You're not wearing it."

"My mom told me to take it off when we have guests over."

Mei had lost her left eye when she was young, and the blue iris of the false eye—the doll's eye that Kirika, the doll maker, had made specially for her daughter—it probably made Kirika sad that Mei hid it behind an eye patch, given that.

"The person on the far right is Mr. Sakaki. He was twenty-four years old when this was taken two years ago."

"Which one is your dad?"

"He's the one who took the picture. So he's not in it."

There was an older couple I presumed was the Hiratsukas and a little girl perched between them. A short distance from the couple, on the far right of the group, a slightly built boy stood next to Teruya Sakaki.

Most of the people getting their picture taken were offering the camera an appropriate smile; Mei and Sakaki were the only two not smiling.

"The boy next to Mr. Sakaki is Sou. Mr. Hiratsuka's wife...her name is Tsukiho. Anyway, that's her son. He was a fourth-year in elementary school that year."

So he's three years younger than Mei and me.

He was a very pale, subdued-looking boy, though not as much as Mei. He had managed a smile for the picture, but there was something forlorn about it. Maybe that was just my imagination.

"Who's the girl?"

"That's little Mirei. She was probably three in this picture. She's Sou's younger sister, but apparently they have different fathers."

"So then..."

"Tsukiho remarried with Mr. Hiratsuka. Mirei is the child she had with him, and Sou is the child of her previous husband. He passed away after Sou was born."

Hrmm. It was kind of convoluted, but not exactly incomprehensible.

"Anyway—"

Mei rested both elbows on the edge of the table and perched her chin on her hands, gazing down at the photo in my hands.

"This was the first time I'd ever met Mr. Sakaki. When someone asked him a question, he would answer, but he didn't start any conversations himself...He was aloof and hard to please. That was my first impression of him."

"He looks a little like Mr. Chibiki, don't you think?"

"I guess."

"Not like how Mr. Chibiki looked when he was younger. He comes across so different in old pictures from how he is now, you know? This is more like if you took Mr. Chibiki the way he is now and made him be in his mid-twenties. I bet if you put glasses on this guy, they'd look even more alike."

"...Maybe."

"So did this Sakaki guy not live with the Hiratsukas?"

"No," Mei replied, taking back the photo. "Mr. Sakaki has always lived by himself in his Lakeshore Manor..."

Placing the photo to one side of the circular table, Mei seemed to hesitate for a moment, then reached out once again to her sketchbook. She opened it to a page in the middle and showed it to me. "This." The drawing was—

A picture of a building.

It was a sketch in pencil, but it looked amazingly artistic for a middle school student to have done.

Against a backdrop of forest or woodland, as far as I could tell from looking at the picture, it was a somewhat large, magnificent house. So this was the Lakeshore Manor Mei had just mentioned.

It was a two-story, Western-style building. The walls had clapboard siding, I think it's called. The windows were basic, tall, and slid open vertically. The roof wasn't a gable exactly, but instead had a shape where two different slopes met. There were also several small windows in a row just a tiny distance above the ground…

"There's another sketch of this same house on the next page."

The composition of this one showed the building from a different angle.

The windows on the second floor were distinctive, different from the rest. They had an elliptical shape with the bottom half cut away at an angle, and there were two of them, on the left and right, in a mirrored pair…They seemed almost like the house's eyes.

"It kinda reminds me of the *Amityville* house, you know?"

I found myself giving voice to this impression. Mei cocked her head slightly in confusion, so I asked, "Have you never seen the movie *The Amityville Horror*? It's the house in that."

A frenzied demon house, at that.

"Never heard of it," Mei replied flatly, her head still tilted to one side.

4

"So this was last summer?"

This question arose because there was a scribble at the bottom right corner of the drawing, saying "8/1997."

"We went to the vacation house around the same time last year, and when I went for a walk around there, I found this building… and I thought it might be interesting to draw it."

Mei gently closed the sketchbook.

"It just happened to be Mr. Sakaki's house."

"So you ran into Mr. Sakaki last year, too?"

"A couple times, yeah."

"While you were drawing those pictures?"

"There, too…But the first time I saw him last year was at the seashore."

"Seashore? But before you called it Lakeshore Manor."

"Yeah. It's at a lake…which is actually not that big. Picture more like a pond."

Mei narrowed her right eye.

"So there's the sea, and then you walk a little ways from the coast through a small forest, and there's a pond. It's called Lake Minazuki…Oh, so I guess it is a lake after all."

Even after her explanation, I couldn't really picture it. But then, I wasn't really familiar with the area.

"Mr. Sakaki had been taking pictures by the sea. I guess that was his hobby. Sou was with him that day, and I was walking by myself along the shore…and so we ran into each other for the first time in a year. He remembered meeting me the year before, too."

"Huh. So you guys talked?"

"A little."

About what? I wanted to ask, but decided not to.

I don't know what it was, but I felt impolite, maybe awkward, asking so many questions, one right after another. I also got the feeling I would get shut down sooner or later—*I hate the way you're interrogating me.*

As it happened, Mei continued on her own.

"Actually, Mr. Sakaki was the one who spoke up first. 'Oh, I see you've got an eye patch on'…"

"Mei, was it? We met last year at Mr. Misaki's house, right?"

Teruya Sakaki walked up to her, his single-lens reflex camera still in his hands, dragging his left leg a little stiffly.

"Are you hurt?" Mei offered.

"Oh, you mean…" had been his reaction, then he nodded slightly and replied, *"I was in an accident a long time ago."*

The injuries he'd sustained in the accident hadn't completely healed, so he still had a limp in his left leg. The accident had happened when he was in middle school. His whole class had been on a bus, and it had gotten hit by a truck...

"What?!"

As I listened, a memory caused my heart to jolt.

"A bus accident in middle school?"

Two years ago, Teruya Sakaki had been twenty-four years old... That's what Mei had said. So this year he was twenty-six. Which meant he'd been in middle school a little over ten years ago...

"...No way," I whispered and sucked in a deep breath. "This Sakaki guy used to live in Yomiyama? Are you saying he went to North Yomi for middle school and was in Class 3 as a third-year, and then...No way..."

"The tragedy of 1987." Mei nodded solemnly. "I thought the same thing when this year's strategy had started and I was listening to Mr. Chibiki tell all his stories about the old disasters. It made me remember what Mr. Sakaki had said."

Eleven years ago—in the spring of 1987, the disaster that befell third-year Class 3 on their class trip—the class had gotten on a separate bus and was headed out of Yomiyama toward an airport outside the city when the accident struck on the way there. The driver of a truck in an oncoming lane was asleep at the wheel and rammed into the bus...That's what Mr. Chibiki had told us.

A total of seven people, students as well as the head teacher, had been killed in the tragedy. Could that really have been the accident that had injured Teruya Sakaki's left leg?

"So, this summer," Mei went on in a quiet voice. "When we went to the vacation house and I saw Mr. Sakaki, I wanted to confirm it with him. I thought it was worth it, if there was even a tiny chance he could tell me something that might be useful."

I can't believe you! I thought and glared straight into Mei's face. How could she do something like that and not tell anyone?

If she had just given me a heads-up even...But I have to acknowledge, it was a very Mei Misaki kind of thing to do.

As always, Mei was utterly indifferent to my high emotion and forged ahead.

"That's what I was thinking when we left, but Mr. Sakaki had already died. At the start of May of this year. So—"

After letting out a short sigh, Mei casually swept aside her bangs and said, "But I wound up being able to talk to his ghost...So, Sakakibara? Do you want to hear more of this story? Or would you rather not stir up the memories?"

"Um..."

I scrunched my eyebrows together for a second and pressed a thumb against my temple. All the while conscious of a slight low-frequency sound resonating somewhere inside my head, *vmm...vmmmmm...*

"I do want to hear about it."

That was my answer. The corners of Mei's mouth pulled into a smirk and she nodded. Then she started to tell her story.

"Mr. Sakaki died this spring. But they still hadn't found his body...He'd become a ghost, and he was looking for it."

Sketch I

What happens to people when they die?
—Hmm?
Do they move on to the afterlife when they die?
Well…who can say?
Do they go to heaven or hell?
Who knows? After all, people just made up heaven and
hell.
So then, when you die, you really just stop existing?
You become nothingness?
…No, I don't think that's what happens.
Really?
Yeah. When people die, I'm sure they…

I

It was around the end of July last year when I ran into that girl at the shore, where the Raimizaki lighthouse is visible. I can't remember the exact date.

Her name was Mei; she was a girl in middle school. I seem to recall that it was the second time I'd met her.

We'd first met a year earlier. The year before last in the early part of August. It was at the dinner party at the Misaki family's vacation home. My sister Tsukiho had invited me.

She spoke barely a word at the party, limiting herself mostly to mouthing formalities. She was such a fair-skinned girl with a slight build. Quiet and seeming a little sad, she didn't look like she was enjoying the get-together that night much at all. That's what I remembered about her.

The most noticeable thing about her at the time was that her left eye was blue. I had heard that her mother, the doll maker, had made a special false eye for her.

That's why.

The color of her eye, the almost fairy blue, had lingered vividly in my mind…

When we saw each other again last summer, I noticed the patch over her left eye and spoke without thinking.

"Oh-ho. She's wearing an eye patch now, eh?" I even went so far as to thoughtlessly add, "Why would she cover up such lovely mismatched eyes?"

My nephew Sou, who'd come to visit, asked me, "What does 'mismatched eyes' mean?"

The same tone he always used, in the pure alto of a little boy, before the voice changed.

"It means her eyes are different colors."

After giving my answer, I walked over to the girl.

"You're Mei, if I recall? We met last year at Mr. Misaki's house."

"…Hello."

She responded in a voice so quiet it was almost swallowed up by the sound of the waves and turned her right eye to look down at my feet.

"Are you hurt?" she asked.

"Oh, you mean…," I began, then looked down at my left leg and nodded slightly. "I was in an accident a long time ago," I replied. "Did you not notice it last year?"

"Er...no."

"My injury never fully healed, so unfortunately I have a slight limp in my left leg now. Not that it hurts, though."

As I spoke, I tapped my left leg just above the knee to demonstrate.

"It was a terrible accident, actually. I was in middle school. The bus my class was on got hit by a truck..."

The girl angled her head slightly, saying nothing.

"Several of my friends died. So did the head teacher. I was one of the survivors," I continued.

Again nothing.

"I'm Teruya Sakaki. Nice to meet you again."

"...Likewise."

"This is my nephew, Sou...But you knew that. He's my sister's— That is, Tsukiho Hiratsuka's son, but when he's on vacation, he often comes to visit me...I'm glad we're so close, but you know, Sou, you need to make some friends at school, too."

Sou didn't react to this, but timidly came out from behind me and greeted the girl. "Hello." Just like the girl, his voice was almost lost in the sound of waves.

A short time later, I felt as if I were rambling endlessly at the girl. About my hobby of taking photos, about the mirages you could see in the ocean here from time to time...

I had a few more opportunities to see and talk to her after that also, but I can't remember the details. I might be able to bring it back in snatches, but maybe not. Nevertheless—

I do remember making a comment along these lines to her at some point: "Your eye. That blue eye."

I said it, knowing full well that it was an artificial eye inserted in place of her natural eye.

"With that eye of yours, you might be seeing the same things I am…looking in the same direction."

At that, she looked back at my face, somewhat startled. "Why?" she whispered. "Why would you…?"

"You know, I'm not sure," I answered, perplexed, unable to formulate anything more than that ambiguous response—that's how it seemed. "I wonder why I said that."

The girl's name is Mei. Mei Misaki.

I had heard that Mei was written with the character for *howl*.

The rumble of a mountain. The boom of a thunderclap. Mei Misaki.

It was about nine months after this that I, Teruya Sakaki, died.

2

I don't mean that I "died" metaphorically. Not "as good as dead" and not "dead at heart."

I died.

I am no longer alive; I am dead. That much is not in question.

Indisputably, I died this spring—one day at the start of May.

I stopped breathing, my heart stopped beating, and my brain activity stopped for all eternity…and I became **what I am now**. An existence without the physical body of a living man, and only the consciousness (…soul?) deemed "I." What you might call a ghost.

I died.

At the beginning of May, getting close to the end of Golden Week. The date was May 3, a Sunday. My twenty-sixth birthday.

It was after eight thirty that night. I believe there was a hazy half-moon blurred into the sky.

I died.

I clearly remember the scene—the sight before me in the very moment that I lost my life, or perhaps just before it slipped away. It forms a vivid picture, complete with a mix of sounds and voices.

I was inside my house. In the spacious foyer with stairs up to the second floor...

I was in the hall of Lakeshore Manor, where I had lived for many years alone. Tsukiho and I had long called this place, doubling as a spacious stairwell, located at the center of the building near the entrance hall, the "grand entry."

I had collapsed on the hard black floor of the grand entry. I wore black pants and a white, long-sleeved shirt. An ensemble not unlike that of a middle school or high school student.

My body lay faceup. My arms and legs were splayed out, bent at jarring angles. I tried to move but failed completely.

My face was turned sideways. As with my arms and legs, I was totally unable to move it. Something must have happened to the bones in my neck...And then there was the blood.

Some part of my head had split open, and red blood smeared my forehead and cheek. A pool of blood was gradually spreading over the floor. It was a terrible scene.

On the threshold of death, my eyes open wide and glassy—one might say **I saw** this picture.

Thinking reasonably, you would never expect to be able to see yourself in such a state with your own eyes. There was a simple **trick** to it.

What I had looked at that day was a mirror hanging on the wall of the room.

A large rectangular mirror taller than a person.

The mirror showed that picture—showed *me*—as I looked in the moments when my life slipped away. As I lay on the brink of death, my eyes were inadvertently locked on it.

The reflection of my bloody face suddenly transformed.

The contorted, taut expression slackened into an oddly peaceful look, as if freed from pain, fear, and uncertainty…And then.

A faint movement on my lips.

Trembling ever so slightly. It was—

Was I **saying something?**

Yes. I **was**…But—

I don't now know what I might have been trying to say at that moment, or whether I did, in fact, say anything. I also don't know what I felt or thought at that time. I can't remember it.

I could hear a sound.

An antique grandfather clock stood in the hall. Its bell chimed once.

It was eight thirty. And as if overlaying that solemn echo—

I could hear a voice.

Someone's voice shouting faintly.

Calling my name ("…*Teruya*…"). Ah. I know this voice.

All at once, I noticed.

The sight of myself in the mirror, slipping away. In one corner of the mirror, I could see the reflected form of the "someone" whose voice I heard. It was…

…

…

…And this is where my living awareness cuts off. It wasn't an out-of-body experience like people talk about so often, but I do believe this was the moment of my death.

Even now, this memory of death lingers so vividly in my mind, but everything before and after is a sprawling blank, as if obscured by a thick fog. The answers to "Why did I die?" or "What happened after I died?" aren't clear. The "after" part of the "before and after" is more than merely blank…it's an unfathomable darkness.

Bottomless, empty…the darkness that follows death.

*   *   *

This is how I, Teruya Sakaki, died.

And why afterward, I began **this existence**—what you might think of as a ghost.

3

When you think about it, it seems obvious, but being a ghost is an extremely unsettling state of being. I've learned this from experience.

Ever since my death that night, I've had an imperfect sense of time.

And of course, since I don't have a flesh body, I have imperfect somatic senses.

I can have thoughts, but the supporting memories are extremely vague…Perhaps it would be more correct to say that they're choppy and vary greatly in intensity.

Nonconsecutive rather than continuous.

Fragmentary rather than complete.

—I suppose that might describe it.

Same with time.

Same with knowledge.

Same with memories. And same with **my consciousness**.

As if I'm preserving "myself," barely keeping my balance, while I do my best to string together the nonconsecutive, the fragmentary. As if it could scatter in all directions at any moment, all of it truly eradicated…

I feel this threat keenly, but agonizing over it serves no purpose. All I can do is accept things **the way they are now**.

Because in any event, I'm still dead.

4

I **woke up** two weeks after my death.

Which of course is not to say that I came back to life. I noticed that I had suddenly been freed from the *darkness* that had sucked me in immediately after I died and that **there was a "me" here.** That's what I mean by "woke up."

At first I didn't know what was going on.

When I woke up, the first thing I became aware of was a certain large, familiar-looking mirror.

The big rectangular mirror hanging in the grand entry. The mirror that had dispassionately shown me drawing my last breath.

All of a sudden, **I could see it.** Only one or two meters away. Meaning—

I was **in front** of the mirror. I felt myself "standing" there. And yet—

The mirror in front of my eyes showed not the slightest reflection of me standing there. Even though it showed everything else around me exactly as it was.

I could sense my body.

I felt that I had arms and legs, my chest, my neck, my head, my face—all there like usual. I could even see and touch them with my own eyes and hands. I was wearing clothes, too. Black pants with a white, long-sleeved shirt. The same clothes I'd worn the night I'd died in this spot...

...That's how **I am present in this place.**

I could be self-aware.

Regardless, the mirror reflected none of this.

What was going on?

Through intense bewilderment and confusion, I finally achieved a proper understanding of the situation.

That I am present in this place.

But not as one of *the living* with a physical body. I am one of *the dead* and have lost my body of flesh.

The body I now felt as "being here" did not actually exist. Neither did the clothes. Surely they were all *afterimages of life* that only I could sense…And that was why. In other words—for some reason, it seemed that I had **woken up** here as what people would call a ghost.

I turned my eyes away from the mirror.

There were no longer any traces of the blood from my death on the floor before me. I suppose someone had wiped it up afterward.

I looked slowly around at my surroundings.

The large antique grandfather clock standing to one side of the door leading to the entranceway, the clock that had sounded its bell right before my death—its hands were now stopped at 6:06. They didn't move. Perhaps there was no one to wind it now that I was dead.

I went up to the second floor.

When I made this movement, I intended to walk up the stairs, but this was presumably also an *afterimage of life*. As, I'm sure, was the fact that I had a slight limp in my left leg when "walking," just as I had in life.

When I reached the second floor, a gallery-like path ran almost halfway around the open hall of the foyer.

My library, bedroom, and other rooms were on the second floor. There were also several empty rooms I had almost never used in the many years I'd lived here…so it seemed that the general information about this manor had stayed with me despite my shift to being a ghost.

Suddenly, partway down the second-floor hallway—

My eyes stopped on the wooden banister running along the side facing the open space of the foyer.

It had been repaired, new wood fitted into it, as if it had broken or cracked. It looked very much as if it had been an emergency repair.

I looked over the banister and down to the first floor.

So it had happened right down there. The place I had crumpled to on the verge of death that night. Meaning—

Had I fallen from this spot just moments earlier? And I had hit my head hard, maybe snapped my vertebrae, too…

I groped fearfully through the blank space in my memory where the thick fog gathered. And then…

…A voice (What are you doing…? Teruya?).

Someone's voice (…Stop it).

Several voices (…Don't worry about it) (You can't…Don't do it!).

It seemed on the verge of coming back to me (…Don't worry about it), and then slipped away.

I moved down the second-floor hallway. I went into one of the rooms.

It was a bedroom.

Moss-colored curtains were drawn over the window, but the light outside shone through a gap between them, dimly lighting the room.

There was a small double bed. The covers were pulled neatly over it. It looked as if no one had used it in a long time.

There was a small clock on the bedside table.

It was a battery-powered digital clock, and unlike the clock in the grand entry, this one was working normally…2:25 P.M. It showed the date, too. Sunday, May 17.

It was while looking at this display that I finally understood that two weeks of time had passed since my death on the night of May 3.

What had happened in this house that night two weeks ago?

Why and what series of events had led me to a death like that?

The thick fog showed no signs of receding.

I remembered that I had died. But I couldn't really remember what had happened before or after that. Even I had to admit that an "amnesiac ghost" was pretty funny, but—

Why had I died?

That was when I decided I would answer this critical question.

My vision crackled apart, like a TV screen with a bad signal. Several images floated before me in that moment.

On the bedside table.

A bottle of something and a glass, and also...

Near the center of the room.

Something white hanging there, swaying...

...What?!

What is this?—by the time the question entered my mind, the images had already vanished.

Confused, I murmured, "What on earth...?"

My ears, nothing more than relics themselves, picked up the "voice" issuing from my throat, nothing more than an *afterimage of life*. In life, my voice had been a rich baritone; hearing the cracking, papery sound that echoed now without any similarity startled me.

Instinctively, both hands went to my throat.

My fingers, only an afterimage, touched my skin, itself an afterimage— *Oh. This* sensation *won't tell me anything. But...*

"My throat," I tried whispering once again.

My voice was indeed hoarse.

My throat must have been crushed when I'd died two weeks earlier. I'd fallen from the second-floor hallway, may have broken my neck...So, even as a ghost, my voice wouldn't...

I lingered there gloomily, and the hollow *darkness* crept back in.

5

Ghosts are said to "appear."

At graves, for example.

At ruins and abandoned houses, for example.

At intersections and tunnels, the frequent subject of rumors...
They **appear**.

From the perspective of the people **to whom a ghost appears**, anything these people lack the basic ability to see or feel normally must be a ghost. When they can see or feel them for some spontaneous reason, people are surprised and say the ghost "appeared," and they're frightened.

People usually can't correctly predict when a ghost will appear. Even when they try, they're often wrong. So most times people are caught unawares. And so they're scared. I suppose that's how it works.

However, now that I'd become a ghost, I believed the situation was pretty much the same for **the one doing the appearing**, too. Meaning that...

A dead person's spirit (their...soul?) lingering in *this world* after death is actually an extremely unnatural and unsettling *state of being*.

It is not continuous.

It is not a definitive ending, but rather a gathering together of fragments, struggling to preserve some sameness.

So—

"I," as a ghost, will not "exist" perpetually at every hour of the day. I don't "exist"; I do in fact "appear."

Absent even this degree of overriding law, without purpose or meaning (so it seemed), from time to time I appear and then disappear. I don't know how it is for ghosts generally, and there's no way I could find out, but that's how it was for me, at least.

I feel like it's not a very apt metaphor, but it can also be understood using the terms *sleep* and *waking*.

When I died and became a ghost, I was usually in the hollow *darkness* I mentioned before, **asleep**. I suppose the *darkness*
might have been a threshold between this world and the next.
And every now and again, I would **wake up** and wander through
this world. In other words, I would "appear."

While I was **appearing**, all I ever thought about was my own
death.

Why did I die?

What happened after I died?

I…

The numerous pressing questions of the amnesiac ghost. In
addition to which—

A feeling of deep *sadness*, as if enveloping me entirely…

What was I so sad about?

That was another big question.

What did I have to be sad about anymore?

The fact that I had died?

The twenty-six years of life before my death?

Or maybe…

6

After I **woke up** on May 17, I've occasionally **appeared** at Lakeshore Manor.

In such times, I wandered alone through a house now devoid of
occupants, and while doing so, I firmed my grip on the gradually
fading outlines of "myself from life"…

*   *   *

Teruya Sakaki.
I was born May 3, 1972, in the town of Yomiyama.
Male. Single. Twenty-six years old at death.
Yes. That is me.

My father's name was Shotaro. Shotaro Sakaki.
He was a talented doctor, but six years ago he suffered a severe illness and passed away. It was an unfortunate thing to happen right before I turned twenty. He was sixty when he died.
My mother's name was Hinako.
She had died suddenly in her mid-forties, much earlier than my father, still young. That happened eleven years ago, during my time in middle school…
My sister Tsukiho was eight years older than me.
Her first husband died quite soon after they were married, and she brought her young son Sou, still one year old, back with her to the family home. That was eleven years ago, too. And then with my mother's death coming so soon after that…As a result, our family decided to leave Yomiyama.
The first place we moved was Lakeshore Manor.

This mansion, built near Lake Minazuki in the small town of Hinami, was originally a vacation home belonging to my father, Shotaro. So you might say our move here eleven years ago was like an emergency evacuation. In fact, we secured a new house in another area the following year and the family moved there.
It was a short while after my father's death that I inherited the house and decided to live here. At the time, I was enrolled at a private university in the prefecture, but I decided to use that opportunity to take a break from school. After two years, I finally dropped out.

After that, I continued living here by myself. I never once held a proper job. It was selfishness enabled by the significant inheritance I received from my father.

"I've been fond of this place for a long time," I remember telling someone. Who was I talking to and when was it?

"Dad liked it here, too. It felt like he would take the slightest excuse to come here by himself and stay for a couple days."

I'd heard that going back decades ago, a wealthy foreigner had built the house in the architectural style of his homeland. My father had just happened to see it and like it, and so he'd decided to buy it.

There was a spacious library in the heart of the first floor, as well, separate from the library on the second floor. Of the thousands of books cluttering the bookshelves (which maybe I should feel bad about), the majority belonged to my deceased father's collection.

When I was brought to this house as a child, I would always spend many long hours in these rooms of books. While they were packed full of "grown-up books" in every type of field, they also contained many comics and novels that a kid could enjoy, too.

After I became the master of the house, my nephew Sou came to visit often, and just as I used to, he treated this collection of books as his own private library. Even though I would have thought it was tough to come over since it took close to thirty minutes to reach here from the Hiratsuka house by bicycle.

Tsukiho fell in love with her current husband Shuji at first sight and married him the year before my father's death. She had just become pregnant with Mirei when I started to live here.

Sou...I appreciated his attachment to me, like I was an older brother, but sometimes it worried me a bit, too. I knew he must have some complex feelings about Tsukiho getting remarried and having a little sister with a different father. He was well behaved and introverted but very smart. That alone was reason enough…

"Will you always live here by yourself, Teruya?" Sou asked me once, though I actually can't remember when. "Aren't you ever going to get married?"

"Well, I don't have anyone *to* marry," I remember answering, half-joking. "Plus, it's a lot easier living by yourself. I like this house, and I…"

I…I remember not knowing where to go from there and closing my mouth. Sou was nodding and looking up at my face the whole time.

7

I wonder how the world reacted to my death. Actually, I wonder if my death on the night of May 3 was made public at all.

These were questions I had begun to ask around the latter part of May.

Already half a month after my death, and here was this house believed to have no occupants. And yet the house itself hadn't died, still felt alive…Perhaps that captures the feeling.

I could hear the sound of the refrigerator running in the kitchen, and once when **I appeared**, I even heard the telephone ringing.

When I heard the telephone in the grand entry ring, I was in the library on the second floor. It weighed on my mind and so I went downstairs, but of course as a ghost, I couldn't have answered the phone.

It was the dock for the cordless phone. It had an answering machine built into it, and after the automated message and the beep, the caller's voice played on the speaker.

"*Hey, Sakaki? It's been a while, just wondering how things are goin'. It's me, Arai.*"

Arai...Would that be with the characters for *new well*? Or for *rough-hewn well*?

Groping through my patchy recollections, I teased out a memory. I was sure I'd had a classmate by that name, a long time ago...

Even though I told Sou, "You have to make other friends," when I was alive—and especially the last few years—I'd had almost no one I would have called a friend.

I don't think I was a radical misanthrope or anything. I was just somehow terrible at keeping a conversation going to match the other person's interest or ease their tension, and I never kept relationships going for long...

"*I'll try calling you back later.*"

Arai went on. I couldn't remember what he looked like at all.

"*I bet you're living the easy life, like always. Still, there's somethin' I'd like to talk to you about...Anyway, if you feel like it, give me a call. Okay?*"

I'm sure that when I was alive, I was seen in the world as "doing whatever he wants, not even holding down a job like a responsible adult." It sounds different when you say "educated man of leisure" instead, but even setting aside the "leisure" part, I myself wondered about the "educated" part.

Sometimes I would take my hobbyist camera and go on aimless expeditions in the car. When I was taking a break from college, I even wandered all the way to the ocean by myself. And to India in Southeast Asia, and I think somewhere in South America, too, once...But...

But they all felt like distant dreams now, all sense of reality diluted out of them.

What had I been seeking on those trips? The feelings I'd had at the time were totally obscure to me now.

Photos I'd taken decorated the mansion here and there. There were photos of the places I'd traveled to, but there were also more than a few taken nearby. There was also a photo where I managed to catch a great photo opportunity at the ocean of a strange mirage.

8

While sitting (or perhaps "with the conviction that I sat" would be a more accurate phrasing) in the chair at the desk in the second-floor library, I would, among other things, run through my memories of when I was alive.

In one area of the large desk sat an old-style dedicated word processor. But in my present state, I lacked the *power* to start it up and use it.

For a ghost with no corporeal body, flipping a power switch on machines like this and using them…It seemed I was fundamentally incapable of such actions. Not to say that it was totally impossible for me to touch or move things: I could open a book or notebook, for example, move a door…Those things weren't beyond me.

I wasn't sure where the line was drawn, but the latter class of physical actions would probably look to *the living* like a spiritual manifestation like a poltergeist. That's the explanation I dreamed up.

"What is this a photo of?" I remembered being asked.

Who had asked me that question? And when?

"On the right there, is that you when you were younger, Mr. Sakaki?"

I at least knew that the other person wasn't Sou. Sou wouldn't call me Mr. Sakaki.

A simple, plain wooden picture frame that stood on the desk in the library. The question was about an old color photo inside the frame.

The picture was still on the desk now.

It showed five young people.

Three boys and two girls. The boy on the right in the picture was definitely me. I was wearing a navy blue polo shirt and had my right hand propped on my hip, smiling. I was holding a brown cane in my left hand, but...

It looked like the picture had been taken somewhere near here. There was a lake in the background. Maybe a commemorative photo taken on the shore of Lake Minazuki?

The date the photo was taken was printed in the lower right corner: "8/3/1987." On the border of the picture frame, someone had handwritten, "Last summer vacation of middle school."

It was true—1987 had been eleven years earlier. The year my mother suddenly passed away and my family left Yomiyama, and this had been the summer vacation of that year...

Third year in middle school. A fifteen-year-old me/Teruya Sakaki.

The other four people...Yes, they were friends from my class and—

"It's a photo that brings back a lot of memories," I think I replied to the question. "Of that memorable summer vacation."

"Oh yeah?" the other person responded offhandedly. "You look like you're having a lot of fun, the way you're smiling in this picture. You look like a totally different person..."

...After playing the memory back to this point, I finally remembered.

That's right. It was that girl.

The girl with mismatched eyes I'd run into again on the

seashore at the end of July last year. When she had come over to this house…

The girl's name was Mei. Mei Misaki.

She said Mei was written with the character for *howling*. Mei Misaki—

Sketch 2

What does it mean to "become an adult"?

—Hm?

When you were little, did you ever think, I want to be a grown-up already!

Hmm...I don't really remember.

What age do you have to be to be a grown-up?

Well, you become a legal adult at age twenty. They used to call that "coming of age," and the adulthood ceremony for boys was held when they were younger than that. Like at age twelve.

Does the beginning of adulthood change in different parts of history?

Different parts of history, different countries, and different communities, yeah.

Huh...

To me, I figure once you're in high school, you're probably an adult. Up to middle school, you're a child. That's how long the compulsory education is, anyway, and you can't get married at that point.

You can get married once you're in high school?

Girls can get married at sixteen and boys at eighteen. That's how it's set up.

Huh...

I

Ghosts are said to "haunt" things.

The object of their haunting can be a specific place, or a person, or sometimes an object.

For example, when a ghost haunts a house, that house becomes a haunted house. When haunting a person, in the worst-case scenario, the afflicted person might be possessed and killed. Like in the *Yotsuya Kaidan*, that famous old ghost story. Perhaps the "cursed treasure" that brings its owner bad luck is another example of haunting an object.

There's plenty of fiction written about ghosts, but none of that is anything more than a product of a living person's imagination. No one knows, or could possibly know, what **an actual ghost** is like.

And although I've actually become a ghost myself now, that still doesn't mean I can talk knowledgeably about ghosts in general. The only thing I know about is **my own situation**…

…Still.

Why did I turn into **this**?

This continues to bother me.

I don't think this happens to all the people who die.

What happens to a person after they die? Do they go to an afterlife, like heaven or hell? Or is nothingness the only thing that was ever waiting for us after death?…I decided to set aside such huge questions.

It's hard to believe that my current in-between state, as unnatural and unstable as it is, could be the norm after death. If the world were so full of ghosts, it would be a big deal…Even as a ghost myself, that's how it seemed to me.

This in-between unnatural and unstable condition must be a rather unique one to assume after death.

And given that—
*Why did I turn into **this**?*
I really couldn't shake this thought. Which is only natural.
Wouldn't you expect there to be some fitting reason or cause behind it? It's impossible to resist the urge to think so.

If I assumed that my/Teruya Sakaki's ghost **was haunting something**—
I had the feeling it was definitely a *place* I was haunting. It was Lakeshore Manor, where I had lived in life and where that life had ended. But—
You might then suppose the only place I could **appear** was this mansion, but that seemed not to be the case. That, too—
It was the night of May 27.
The first time I **appeared** anywhere other than Lakeshore Manor.

2

…In a large room facing a veranda.
What had originally been a Japanese-style tatami room had been largely renovated into an imitation of a Western-style combo living and dining room. A high-quality carpet was spread over the floor, on which were arranged a black-painted dining room table and chairs. Several plates and bowls piled with food were set on the table. A table set for dinner.
Three of *the living* were in this place at the time.
Tsukiho Hiratsuka—i.e., my sister.
Her two children—i.e., the older brother Sou and the little sister Mirei.

The image of the three of them sitting around the dinner table was reflected in the glass of the door to the veranda. **Suddenly, I realized I was looking at it.**

After a brief moment of bewilderment, I realized *Aha.* For some reason, without warning, this time I had **appeared here**, somewhere other than Lakeshore Manor.

"Here" being the Hiratsuka house, where Tsukiho lived.

Although also in Hinami, the house was in the long-standing town center, rather far from the Lakeshore Manor built in the vacation home/resort area. But I had visited it several times during my life. I also remembered this combo living and dining room.

Why had my/Teruya Sakaki's ghost suddenly manifested **here**—in the Hiratsuka house—tonight?

The glass door acted as a mirror, reflecting the three figures of the mother and her children. There was no other human figure visible in it. Regardless—

I was positive **I was there**.

By myself to one side of the dining room table. From there, I took in the sight of the room.

I watched the three people's faces and movements.

I listened to their voices and conversation. And yet—

Not a single one of them noticed my presence there. To them, *the living*, the figures of *the dead* (a ghost) were fundamentally invisible.

A clock hung on the wall.

It was seven thirty P.M. The night was already dark outside.

The clock also showed the date.

Wednesday, May 27.

May 27…Ah yes. I'm sure that was the date.

I slowly dredged a memory back up.

Today, I was sure, was Tsukiho's…

"Mommy, Mommy!" Mirei said to Tsukiho. "Where's Daddy? Where's Daddy?"

"Daddy's at work, honey," Tsukiho answered gently.

"At work? Why is Daddy always at work?"

"His work is very important. That's why."

Simply put, Shuji Hiratsuka, whom Tsukiho had married seven years earlier, was a businessman from an old family of the area. He was a **hotshot** who had broadened the business from its origins in real estate and construction.

He was a full twelve years older than Tsukiho, but for some reason he had chosen her for his spouse, despite the fact that she'd already been married and had a child. The details of that were none of my business.

"But today is your birthday, Mommy," Mirei said.

She would be six this year. She was a young child not yet in elementary school, but she already had a surprising command of the words she spoke.

"He's not going to celebrate it with us?"

That's right—May 27 is Tsukiho's birthday, and also…

"But we always celebrate together," Mirei persisted. "We do it for Daddy's birthday, and my birthday, and Sou's birthday. We put candles in a cake and sing 'Happy Birthday' to you…"

"That's true. But today is a little different. Daddy can't come home."

"Whaaat?" Mirei sounded unhappy. "What about the cake? Are we having cake?"

"Oh, I'm sorry, honey. I didn't buy any cake today."

"Whaaaaat?" Mirei looked even more unhappy.

To one side, Sou stayed silent through it all. I couldn't see his face from where I was, and so I looked at his expression in the reflection of the glass door.

I suppose his face could be called expressionless.

It could also be taken as dispirited, and he looked as if he were intently hidden away in a shell…

"What about Uncle Sakaki?" Mirei asked Tsukiho. "Last year Uncle Sakaki came and celebrated with us, right?"

"Oh..."

At that, Tsukiho showed some faint dismay.

"You're right, he did. But Teruya said he can't come today, either. I think he went on a trip somewhere recently."

Went on a trip? She can't mean that—

I died that night!

I died, and now I'm here. I became a ghost and **appeared** here.

I wanted to argue, but I abandoned the idea almost right away. Even if I were to "give voice" to these thoughts and say them aloud, no one would be able to hear me.

A TV standing on a media cabinet was turned on. It looked like a fantasy anime for girls was playing, and finally Mirei turned her attention to that and stopped sulking.

Sou stayed expressionless and silent the whole time. He wasn't even particularly touching his food.

"Are you all right, Sou?" Tsukiho asked him worriedly. "You don't want to eat any more?"

"...No," Sou replied in a quiet voice I wasn't quite sure I actually heard. "...May I be excused?"

"Do you feel up to going to school tomorrow?"

At this new question, Sou shook his head slightly from side to side, not speaking.

3

When Tsukiho finished clearing the table, she spread a newspaper over it and began reading.

Mirei was quietly watching TV.

Sou was sprawled on the sofa in the living room but was still as silent as ever, with nothing resembling an expression on his face...

None of the three showed the slightest sign of noticing my presence in the room.

No matter how I chose to act right now, none of them would see me, and no matter what I said, none of them would hear. It sounds obvious, but now that I had become **like this**, I was simply *not there* to them.

Even so—

Why had Tsukiho said that I "went on a trip"?

I had lost my life in the grand entry of Lakeshore Manor the night of May 3. I had fallen from the second-floor corridor and died. And yet—

Did Tsukiho not know that?

No. She had to know.

Tsukiho must have known.

She must have known that I'd died there that night…(What are you doing…? Teruya?)

When I had looked over the hall railing that showed signs of having been broken and down at the first floor, a memory had seemed to swell back up in my mind. Several voices I had heard that night (…Stop it) (You can't…Don't do it!).

I thought that yes, that had been Tsukiho's voice.

And the other voice answering her (…Don't worry about it) had probably been my own.

Meaning—

On the night of May 3, Tsukiho must have been there and witnessed my death. So then why…?

It wasn't just Tsukiho.

I went to stand beside Sou, who was sprawled out on the sofa, and looked down at his face.

Sou—you were there, too, that night…

"…Whatever," Sou murmured. He said it with such perfect timing that it seemed as if my thoughts had reached him and he had responded to it.

"I don't know about it. I don't know anything. About anything…"

"What's wrong, Sou?"

Tsukiho looked over at him in surprise.

"What's wrong? Why are you…saying those things?"

It must have looked to her as if he had started muttering to himself for no reason.

Without answering, Sou got up from the sofa. He walked over to the table and turned his gaze down to the newspaper Tsukiho had spread open on the table.

At this point, a relatively large headline in the local news section caught my eye.

ACCIDENT KILLS YOMIYAMA NORTH MIDDLE GIRL

That's what the headline said.

"Wha—? What happened?" Tsukiho's dismayed reaction. "This article? What about it?"

She had just tilted her head to one side when a weary "oh" escaped her.

"Yes, Teruya used to go to Yomiyama North Middle…"

Tsukiho turned back to face Sou.

"Did Teruya tell you about it?" she asked. But—

Sou remained silent and only gave an ambiguous tilt of his head.

4

The article in the morning edition on May 27.

ACCIDENT KILLS YOMIYAMA NORTH MIDDLE GIRL

The "accident" announced in this headline transpired as follows.

It happened the previous day, May 26, in the middle of mid-term exams. A third-year student, Yukari Sakuragi, was notified that her mother had been in a car accident and was hurriedly leaving school when she fell down a stairwell of the building, sustaining major injuries that led to her death. The same night, her mother also passed away at the hospital, which she had been transported to.

Reading this article, if Tsukiho or perhaps Sou had sensed something more in this straightforward announcement of an unfortunate accident...

The main reason would have been the name of the school: Yomiyama North Middle. And then the fact that the dead student was a third-year student. It would probably have been these two things.

As Tsukiho said, I had once gone to the same Yomiyama North Middle (abbreviated "North Yomi"). Eleven years ago when my family and I had left Yomiyama, I had been a third-year in Class 3, and...

...I remembered.

My memories of it still remained. I could remember it clearly.

The secret passed on to third-year Class 3 at that school. The undeserved calamities that befall those *with ties* to the class.

Tsukiho, too, had remembered. While reading the article over again, she must have noticed the school name and realized the connection.

But what about Sou?

"Did Teruya tell you about it?" Tsukiho had asked, and I would have expected Sou to answer yes to the question. Yes, I remembered telling him **the story** at some point.

All the times I had told Sou stories of my youth when he had come over to visit, despite the not-insignificant hesitation I felt, still I had...

"You moved out of Yomiyama because of that?" Sou had asked me that day, his face slightly fearful.

"Yes...I suppose we did," I think I replied, lowering my eyes. "We were scared. I was, and so was my father. So we ran. We ran from Yomiyama and moved here."

5

Since that night, I had started to occasionally **appear** places other than Lakeshore Manor.

Sometimes inside the Hiratsuka house where Tsukiho and the children lived, sometimes places nearby in their neighborhood that I remembered. Even at Lakeshore Manor, my **appearances** weren't limited to inside the house. During daylight hours, I might leave the building and go for a walk in the yard, or I might suddenly **appear** in the woods nearby or on the shore of Lake Minazuki.

And there was a fact that I discovered for myself while all this was going on.

Apparently it was not yet acknowledged in the wider world that I/Teruya Sakaki was dead.

My death on May 3 had not been made public. The situation was being treated as if I were still alive and had wandered off on a trip somewhere, just as Tsukiho had told Mirei.

What did this mean?

I had definitely died that night.

I had died and become this ghost.

And yet, the world at large didn't know I had died. Why was that?

There was only one answer I could think of. Namely—

A cover-up.

6

"…How is that going? All right?" Shuji Hiratsuka asked.

"…Yes," Tsukiho answered in a low voice. "For now…I think it is."

"The story is that he went off on a trip by himself, correct?"

"Yes. That's what I've been saying."

"And everything is all right at his mansion, too?"

"The utility bills are automatically drafted from his bank, so there shouldn't be any problems for now…Same with the phone. I told the newspaper some story, and they stopped the deliveries, too…"

"No one in the neighborhood goes by there. And he doesn't really have any friends who would drop by."

"…No."

It was right at the start of June, one night when I **appeared** in the Hiratsuka house, that I overheard this discussion between husband and wife. I had been walking by myself down a long, dark hallway of their sprawling old home and happened to pass by the sitting room where the two were talking.

Hearing their conversation through a sliding paper door, I came to an abrupt stop and strained to listen. Now I was a ghostly eavesdropper, I supposed.

"…How is Sou looking?"

That was Shuji asking. Even with his much younger wife, he spoke in this polite way.

After a short sigh, Tsukiho replied, "Still the same. He's practically shut himself up in his room. Sometimes I call for him and he won't come out…"

"Well, I suppose there will be no helping that for a bit."

"But when I ask him about what happened that night, he tells me, 'Whatever.' Or 'I don't know what you're talking about' or 'I don't remember.'"

"—Is that so?"

Shuji Hiratsuka was a businessman, but on the other hand, he'd had an unorthodox career, having once studied at a medical university and becoming qualified as a physician. In that way, he had maintained a connection with his late father Shotaro, who had been a talented doctor. Apparently that had been the connection that brought him and Tsukiho together.

"He doesn't appear to be getting weaker physically, is that correct?"

"—No."

"I'll look for a good opening and have a talk with him myself. If necessary, there's a specialist I'm on good terms with, so I can consult with him."

"It must have been such a shock to Sou…"

"Of course it would be. But…we're agreed, are we not, Tsukiho? You do understand?"

"—Yes. I understand."

My eavesdropping had led me from the doubts I'd been harboring toward conviction.

Despite knowing about my/Teruya Sakaki's death, they—at the least, Shuji and Tsukiho Hiratsuka—were trying to keep others from learning of it. For some reason, they were trying to cover up what had happened on the night of May 3.

7

My/Teruya Sakaki's death was being covered up.

It was being hidden from the public eye.

Which of course would mean that no funeral had been held, and my corpse had not been cremated or interred.

—So then what?

The question rose up unavoidably at this point.

What had happened to me after my life had ended in the grand entry of Lakeshore Manor on the night of May 3? What had been done to me—or rather, **to my corpse?** Where had it been taken, and what state was it in now?

When I started thinking about such things—

I began to think that the reason I had turned into **this** after my death might lie **there.**

A corpse given no funeral rites and left unburied after death.

A corpse whose current condition and whereabouts were unknown even to (the ghost of) its former occupant.

...That was why.

Because of such a unique situation, I must have gotten stuck in this world after my death in this unnatural and unstable existence.

In which case...

If that were the case, then I...

8

"You know, this lake is half-dead."

I remembered having this conversation.

It was mid-June. I spoke spontaneously, while standing on the bank of Lake Minazuki and gazing for a long while out at its deep green surface.

"You could say it's a double-bottomed lake. The water quality is divided into an upper and lower layer—a shallow layer and a deep layer. The upper layer is fresh water, and the lower layer is brackish."

"What's 'brackish'?"

The person I was talking to cocked their head slightly.

I explained that brackish water was low-concentration salt water created by mixing fresh water with seawater.

"Salt water is heavier, so it sinks to the bottom, and over years and years, the oxygen in it dissipates completely. Plants and animals can't live in deoxygenated water. So the bottom half of the lake is a world devoid of life. That's why the lake is half-dead."

"Half...dead."

The other person repeated those words.

And then **she** carefully removed the white eye patch that covered her left eye. Yes—the other person was that girl: Mei Misaki. We had been talking, gazing out at the lake surface from this place on the shore.

"Hey," I said, seeing her movement. "Why are you taking off your eye patch?"

"—Just felt like it," she answered curtly.

She wore a woven straw hat with her summery white dress. Red sneakers on her feet. A small rucksack was slung over her shoulder, and she held a sketchbook under her arm. Her outfit came vividly back to me.

It was...last summer.

I think it was at the beginning of August. A couple days after we'd met on the beach at the end of the previous month. Sou had come over to visit me, and he spotted her with her sketchbook open where she had installed herself in the shade of the trees beside Lakeshore Manor. She said she hadn't known it was my house, that she had been wandering the neighborhood and found the house by chance and had wanted to try drawing it, or something along those lines.

I had gone out to the lakeshore, so Sou brought her over to me...

"Do you like drawing? Are you in the art club at your school or anything?"

The girl didn't answer any of these questions, but ran her eyes over the surface of the lake and said, "I had no idea there was a lake this close to the ocean."

"You didn't know about it?"

She didn't answer.

"There are two other lakes near here actually. Together they're called the Three Lakes of Hinami. They're pretty famous."

She had nodded slightly but continued to scan the surface of the lake, and so I'd said to her: "This lake is half-dead, you know."

9

"I like this better than the ocean."

I recall Mei Misaki saying that at the time. I had remembered it.

Early in the midsummer afternoon. But the sky was slightly cloudy and the sunlight was gentle. A breeze blowing in off the lake added a chill.

"Why?" I asked.

"People always say, 'But the ocean's right over there...' Very few people bother coming here to relax. If anything, this is an unpopular, neglected spot."

"The ocean—" As she responded, Mei slowly closed and then opened both eyes, her right and her left. "The ocean is too full of living creatures. So I prefer this."

"Hmm."

And—yes—I'm pretty sure it was after that when, a short while later, I said these words to her: "Your eye. That blue eye."

With her eye patch off, I was looking at the strange blue of her false eye.

"With that eye of yours, you might be seeing the same things I am…looking in the same direction."

"Why?" She was the one to ask the question this time. "Why would you…?"

"You know, I'm not sure." I could only offer this ambiguous response. "I wonder why I said that."

After a pause, she murmured, "If you're like me…then I'm not sure that would be a good thing."

"And why is that?" I followed with another question, and reaching up to lightly cover the blue iris of her left eye with her hand, she shook her head quietly.

"…It just is."

Mei Misaki.

I had heard she was a second-year middle schooler living in Yomiyama. Meaning that this summer would mark the start of her third year…

I wondered which school she went to.

The thought started to bother me, and almost simultaneously I shuddered as a chill went down my spine. Even as a ghost.

Was it possible—that her middle school was Yomiyama North Middle? And was it possible that she would be in Class 3?

That she was in the same class as that student, Yukari Sakuragi, whose death had been reported in the newspaper?…

…

…

"…It's not impossible," I muttered to myself in a rasping croak of a *voice*.

Sketch 3

Do you want to grow up? Or would you rather not?
…Whichever.
"Whichever"?
You're not free as a kid…But I hate grown-ups.
You hate them?
It depends on the person. If I could be a grown-up I
like, I'd want to grow up right now.
Ah, I see. But you know, it isn't that great being grown-up.
It isn't?
I wish I could go back. To being a kid.
Why?
…
Why do you want to go back to being a kid?
…Because I want to remember it, I suppose.
Remember what?
Oh, well…

I

June passed and July began…The seasons turned toward summer, and all sorts of things changed in all sorts of ways as time rolled on, while I remained unchanged.

In this unnatural, unstable "state of existence" as a ghost, continuing to linger noncommittally in the *world of the living* in a half-formed way, every once in a while **appearing** without any set cycle or regularity.

At Lakeshore Manor or somewhere nearby.

In the Hiratsuka house or that neighborhood.

I also appeared in places that didn't fall into any of those categories. On a seaside path on a rainy day or on the grounds of a dilapidated temple whose name I didn't know…

And yet no one noticed these frequent apparations. Not a single person.

What could possibly be the reason I had **become this way**?

I felt as if I already knew the answer to this question. I wouldn't say I was 100 percent positive, but it seemed plausible.

I don't think, for example, that I held a grudge against someone or that I held on to some lingering attachment or regret about some task that I had failed to complete. Even as an amnesiac ghost, I would expect to have at least a tiny awareness of it if such strong emotions were at the root of this—and yet.

I felt no malice toward anyone in particular.

And I didn't have any good guesses about what I might have left unfinished—I don't think.

All I had was a feeling of *sorrow* overlying my entire self, profound and yet undefinable…

…That's why.

Thinking about it, I feel sure the cause is the fact that I remain "unmourned."

I died, but my death is unacknowledged by anyone, and no funeral or proper burial has taken place. Not only that, but not even I know where my physical body (read: corpse) is or what happened to it after I died. In such an unjust situation, I suppose I will continue on **this way**.

Which would mean…

2

When I **appear** somewhere, even if I try to touch someone, they never realize I'm there. I suppose some people might get *a feeling*, but it isn't clear-cut.

Ghosts have a lot of problems—is that really what this boils down to?

Suppose I was a vengeful spirit with a violent malice at the root of my existence: I would probably haunt the person I hated and end up trying to kill them. I suppose that sort of ghost has characteristics that make it easy to detect its presence, i.e., easy to spot. These are examples of the pointless things I wound up thinking about.

In my case, I was presumably a different kind of ghost. In basic terms, no one was aware of me or saw me. To say nothing of the fact that I wasn't trying to haunt or kill anyone specific, not that I even could. No matter where, when, or how I appeared, I was utterly "not there" to people.

All I could do anymore was accept it and think, *So that's how it is...* As July started, the feeling of surrender was gaining ground inside me.

For example, I thought about possibly kicking up a fuss reminiscent of a poltergeist to draw attention. But even if I was to try that, I don't think my message (Teruya Sakaki died and turned into a ghost, and I'm right here!) would come across very clearly. It seemed like it would just get confused for petty tricks. I felt worthless. Of course Sou and Mirei wouldn't get it, nor would Tsukiho or Shuji, who seemed to be covering up my death...

There was only one avenue left to me now.

Something that might have some meaning if I tried it. That being—

To find my body, presumably.

My body, which had fallen to its death in the grand entry of Lakeshore Manor on the night of May 3. My body, whose death I knew had not been properly mourned and which I knew had not been properly buried.

Where was it now? What state was it in? *If I could just find that out...*, I thought.

If I could just find that out and see the body for myself, to be able to directly experience my own *death* in a *form* so undeniable...

If I could do that, then maybe.

Maybe then I would be freed from my current *existence*.

3

That being the case—

I started to conduct *a search for my body* each time I **appeared**.

I didn't imagine **it** would be at the Hiratsuka house or anywhere nearby. The place it seemed most likely to be was Lakeshore Manor or the surrounding area.

With that in mind, I decided that every time I **appeared**, I would search every conceivable hiding spot with purpose.

First up was everywhere inside the house.

Each room on the first and second floors. In the attic and in the basement. The bathrooms and powder rooms, of course, as well as storerooms and closets and inside various wardrobes. The ability to exert physical influence seemed to depend on the time and location, and there were limits on the range and extent of that influence, but I was able to open and close doors and drawers without difficulty.

There were several rooms with locked doors on the second

floor, but these posed no problems to me since I lacked a physical flesh-and-blood body. The mere desire to enter brought me inside. I also went to the attic and basement. I even peered into the depths of an old fireplace that had long gone unused. Nevertheless—

In the end, my body was nowhere to be found within the house…

The next place I looked was the garage built on the grounds, adjacent to the house.

Ever since becoming a ghost, I had yet to go back into the garage. On its face, it was a one-story "shed" made of wood with a time-worn appearance, which I had used in life to park my car and store my tools.

The car was still there, as I had left it.

It was a white station wagon that I won't claim was cared for impeccably. I didn't own a moped or bicycle. One reason being the old wound to my left leg, so I had only ever used four-wheeled vehicles.

The car wasn't locked, and the key was hanging on a pegboard in the garage. Just as I had done in life.

The driver's seat, the passenger seat, the backseat, the storage space…in all it was the same: My body wasn't there.

I searched every nook and cranny of the garage, including under the car. But still I found nothing…

It wasn't in the building.

So then outside, I suppose. In which case, the boundaries expanded endlessly.

The front and backyards on the property. The surrounding woods. The lakeside. It could even be in the ground or in the lake. Even leaving aside the forest, there was always the ocean. Thinking about it sent me into a tailspin.

I had nothing resembling a clue to follow.

In essence, this was an issue tied to "what happened there on the night of May 3 after Teruya Sakaki died?" As it happened, even after becoming a ghost, the very same Teruya Sakaki/I didn't know. The situation was utterly absurd. The *blank*, like a thick fog rising over the events before and after my death, I continued to regard with bitterness—

I reviewed my questions.

Why had I died in the first place?

What had happened after I died?

Since these questions remained just that, there were limits on what I could do. At least I could try expanding the range of my *search*, centering on Lakeshore Manor…

On the other hand, I also had a sense that, well, there isn't any particular rush about it, either.

Because it wasn't going to change the fact that I was dead.

Of course, I wouldn't call my current state a pleasant one, but nor did I have any confidence about what might happen if I were to find my body. I could handle the vague idea of it, but when I considered whether or not it was what I truly wanted, I became somehow uncertain…

…Still.

"When a person dies, I feel like they can connect in some way with everyone."

Ah…what is this?

Oh yes, this is something I said to someone sometime in the past.

"Who is 'everyone'?"

When they asked me that, I believe I answered, "I mean everyone who died before them."

…And yet.

Even though I was dead, I was completely alone here. Stranded in this unnatural, unstable existence.

*I don't want to be **like this** forever*—I know that some part of me felt this way, too.

4

As it neared the middle of July, I happened to be there again when the phone in the grand entry rang.

"Sakaki? Hellooo? You still not there?"

After the machine picked up, a man's voice I remembered hearing before played on the speaker.

"It's me, Arai. Have you been gone this whole time or what? I guess you didn't get my other messages."

I got them two months ago…but, well.

His tone implied *I tried calling a couple other times, you know.* Although certainly I seemed to recall that in that call two months ago, it sounded like there was something he wanted to talk about.

"I guess you're on a long trip? That would be a major problem for me. I can't remember if you have a cell phone or not. I hope you can try and pick up on this SOS from an old buddy."

Wish I could, but…sorry, there's not much I can do about it now. Not to mention that the way I am now, I still can't really remember what this "old buddy" even looks like.

"I say it's an SOS, but well, kind of like that other time, I was hoping you could help me out. After all, back in northyomi (?), we went through it all together…Right?"

I thought, *Wha—?*

We went through it all in northyomi?

I guessed "northyomi" was "North Yomi." Yomiyama North Middle abbreviated to North Yomi. Where I had gone until partway through my third year, eleven years ago…

So Arai was a classmate from back then?

From North Yomi…in third-year Class 3 that year?

"Anyway, when you get this, could you call me? Please, Sakaki, babe."

Once he hung up, I went straight to the library on the second floor.

An old friend named Arai...I still couldn't remember if his name was written with the characters for *new well* or *rough-hewn well*, but I thought maybe...

The photo standing on my desk in the library...the commemorative one taken during the summer break of 1987. Maybe one of the people in that photo is him, I thought.

5

They say it started in 1972.

Twenty-six years ago looking back from today and fifteen years ago looking back from when I was a third-year in middle school eleven years ago.

At the start of that school year, a student named Misaki in third-year Class 3 of North Yomi died.

Misaki was a popular kid, beloved by everyone. None of the students wanted to accept such a sudden death, and...

"They said, 'Misaki isn't dead. Misaki is still alive, sitting in the classroom **right over there**.' All of them started to **pretend** like that was true. The head teachers did it, too, and they kept **the act** up all the way to graduation apparently."

I remembered telling Sou about the old legend.

It was after graduation that strange things started to happen. They say that the figure of Misaki, who couldn't possibly have been there in reality, showed up in the class's group photo taken in the classroom after the graduation ceremony.

"A photo of a ghost?" I remembered Sou asking, his head cocked.

"Something like that, anyway. Although I never saw the photo myself," I replied before continuing with the story.

"They say that became the trigger. And the year after that, strange...or I should say, terrifying things started happening in third-year Class 3."

It didn't happen every year. There seemed to be "on years" and "off years," and in an "on year," the number of people in the class would go up by one without anyone ever noticing. No one could tell who the "extra person" was. There wouldn't be enough desks and chairs at the start of the semester, so they could tell the number of people had increased. And then—

"In years where an extra person was in the class, calamities would befall the class."

"Calamities?"

"It means misfortunes, or accidents. In other words...people would die. Every month, someone related to that year's third-year Class 3..."

Whether it was an accident, or an illness, or suicide...There were many **ways to die**, but every month at least one person with ties to the class would die. People with ties to the class included the students and head teacher and also included their close relatives. This would continue until the day of the graduation ceremony.

"Was that—?"

Even when I explained, at first Sou cocked his head in confusion again.

"Was it a curse?"

"A curse...Well, some people say it is. But it doesn't mean that the extra person who infiltrates the class is the vengeful spirit of the student named Misaki. According to the legend, the extra person is supposed to be a casualty...someone who died in a previous year's disaster. But that person doesn't do anything bad themselves. So I think it's a little different from a normal curse."

"Did that—?" Sou looked more and more troubled. "Did that happen for real?"

"Have I ever lied to you, Sou?"

"But..."

"It really happened." I replied with a serious face. "I experienced **it** myself eleven years ago. In third-year Class 3 at North Yomi..."

The number of desks and chairs in the classroom was wrong, and there was a group of people who started panicking about it being an on year...In April, first one student's grandmother died. But since that was the death of an elderly person caused by illness, there were a significant number of skeptics who treated it as **an unfortunate coincidence**. But then—

"At the start of May, we had our school trip, and as the bus was heading to the airport, just before we left the city limits of Yomiyama, the bus got in a huge accident."

At that, I pointed to my left leg, which still bore the scars of the injury I'd sustained in that accident. A short gasp escaped Sou. His expression transformed from confusion to terror.

"Several of my classmates died in that accident. So did the head teacher, who was riding with us. We were all...everyone in the bus was covered in blood...It was a terrible accident."

I sighed and slowly shook my head. Sou was looking at me wide-eyed, as if he might start crying at any moment.

"I was hurt badly enough to be hospitalized, and it took a whole month before I could leave. But when I was finally able to go to school, the disaster next struck my own family. You were only a year old, so you wouldn't remember what happened in the middle of June that year..."

My mother Hinako's death.

She had gone shopping by herself and suddenly collapsed, and by the time she was transported to the emergency room, it was already too late. The cause of death was listed as heart failure, but according to my father Shotaro, she had been in perfect health.

He couldn't believe she would die so suddenly and became skeptical. Of course, he grieved and was filled with sorrow, too.

I had been unable to say anything before, but faced with that, I revealed the secret of third-year Class 3 to my father. Breaking the commandment passed on to the class—that indiscriminately telling other people about it would bring worse calamity down on us.

I suppose the bus accident in May and my mother's sudden death in June were both disasters visited on third-year Class 3. I'm sure of it.

If the legend of the class were true, then the disasters weren't over yet. Someone with ties to the class would die the next month, and the month after that, and the month after that…all the way until graduation. It could be me or my family—maybe my father or my older sister Tsukiho.

"My father—your grandfather—was a doctor, and doctors are scientists, so he didn't believe me right away. But I begged him so desperately…and I'm sure with the bus accident and my mother's sudden death, even my father couldn't help but feel something abnormal was going on…"

"Is that why you moved away from Yomiyama?" Sou asked, his eyes wide.

"That's right," I replied, lowering my gaze.

"We were scared. My father and I both were. So we ran. We fled Yomiyama and moved here."

When I transferred schools and the family left Yomiyama, then of course we would be able to escape the disasters. That's what we thought. So…

We cleared out of our house in Yomiyama and moved here to Lakeshore Manor, like an emergency evacuation. That was right after the start of July.

That month, one of the students in third-year Class 3 at North Yomi jumped off the roof of the school building and died.

6

Last summer break of middle school

These words were written on the old color photo in the standing frame. I stood in front of the desk on which it rested, gazing down at it once again—

"What is this a photo of?"

I remembered being asked this question last summer, in this same spot, by that girl—Mei Misaki.

"On the right there, is that you when you were younger, Mr. Sakaki?"

Five people standing with the lake in the background.

Facing the picture, the boy on the far right with his hand on his hip was definitely me. On the date printed in the photo—"8/3/1987"—a fifteen-year-old Teruya Sakaki.

"It's a photo that brings back a lot of memories," I said in answer to her question. "Of that memorable summer vacation."

"Oh yeah?" she responded offhandedly. "You look like you're having a lot of fun, the way you're smiling in this picture. You look like a totally different person…"

I'm sure I do, I now remember thinking at the time. Because I don't think I smile this way very much now that I'm an adult.

"It's because I was with really good friends," I think I answered at the time. "We were all classmates in middle school."

…Yes.

That's right: Everyone in this photo, we were all friends in third-year Class 3 that year at North Yomi…

"My dad took the picture for us," I remembered adding, though she hadn't asked.

"Grandpa was there?"

A voice came from one side. It was Sou.

I recalled that, unusually, Tsukiho had brought both Sou and Mirei over to visit that day. I could hear the sounds of Mirei frolicking with her mother downstairs.

"Yup," I replied, turning to look at Sou. "Back then, Grandpa lived in this house, too, and so did you. Although you were just a baby."

"Did Mom live here, too?"

"Of course she did. It must have been hard for her looking after you back then."

I seem to remember that the girl listened to us talk in silence, her right eye, without its eye patch, crinkling with a smile.

7

I looked anew at the commemorative photo taken during the summer break eleven years ago. Then I ran through the faces and outfits of the four people in the photo other than myself.

Two boys and two girls.

The two boys were on the left side, and the two girls were on the right side. I/Teruya Sakaki was standing on the right edge of the group with a noticeable gap between the two girls and me. I was holding a cane in my left hand, probably because the injuries to my leg still hadn't healed three months after the accident.

The boy on the left was tall and lanky and was wearing a gaudy Hawaiian shirt, exuding an unmistakable air of "off to summer holiday!" He had his right hand thrust forward with a thumbs-up and was grinning broadly.

Beside him, a boy wearing a blue T-shirt was comparatively short and chubby, his face ridiculously serious behind his silver-rimmed glasses. His arms were crossed in front of his chest, and his lips were twisted a little grouchily.

One of these two was the Arai who'd called me. But which one was it?

I stared at their faces.

Then I reached out for the picture frame with both hands and tried to gently pick it up. It lifted. Exerting this level of influence over an object this size wasn't difficult.

I felt like the impression I'd gotten from his voice and way of talking matched the Hawaiian shirt kid on the left more. But... argh, I don't know. I couldn't remember which of them was Arai, nor the name of the one who wasn't Arai.

I shifted my gaze to the two girls.

The one on the left wore a light blue blouse with a tight, white skirt. She, too, was short and wore silver-rimmed glasses, but her short haircut and delicate features seemed to suit her. She was flashing a peace sign and smiling slightly, but her expression betrayed a trace of nervousness.

The girl on the right was slender and about the same height as I'd been at the time, dressed in denim pants and a beige shirt. She was holding down her long hair, which was being teased by the wind, while also flashing a peace sign with a relaxed smile...

...No, I still had no idea.

I returned the frame to its spot and lowered myself into the chair at the desk. I slumped against the back of the chair.

These people had been good friends of mine, and yet...And yet I could remember nothing about them. Not their names, or personalities, or their voices, or how they talked.

"It's a photo that brings back a lot of memories."

The words I had spoken in response to a question from Mei Misaki that day last summer echoed very distantly, somehow hollow, in my ears that were themselves nothing more than a "relic of life."

8

I casually opened a drawer of the desk without any particular purpose.

My eye happened to fall on something while I slumped in the chair, and truly unintentionally, I reached out a hand toward it. It was the lowest, deepest drawer.

Several partitions divided the interior, in one section of which rested a row of several thick notebooks. The notebooks...No, they were store-bought diaries. Seven-by-ten daily planners sold at bookstores and stationery stores toward the end of every year.

They were arranged in the drawer with their spines upward. The spines were printed to read, for example, "Memories 1992"...

...That's right. I remembered now.

I had started keeping a diary every year in this room. I did it when the mood struck me or when it seemed necessary, and the majority of it was dashed-off notes, so writing by hand had been much more convenient than starting up the computer.

The first volume was from six years ago. The year my father passed away and I inherited this mansion and took up residence here.

That was *Memories 1992*, followed by *Memories 1993*, *Memories 1994*, and so on in order.

I thought, *If I could pick these up and read them...*

All the different memories that I had lost or that had faded since I became a ghost might come back a little bit…But no.

Before that, I need to— I thought, peering into the drawer.

First would be the new diary.

May 3 of this year, the day I died. If I had written something down before that night, then I might find a clue to why I died.

As it happened—

I couldn't find that crucial volume, *Memories 1998*, in the drawer.

…Why not?

I was stymied for a moment and looked around the room.

Maybe on the desk? No.

The bookshelves on the walls, which were full of books and notebooks. Maybe there? No.

I opened all the other drawers in the desk, too. But I couldn't find the planner for 1998 in any of them…

Maybe I hadn't been keeping a diary for this year? But why wouldn't I be? I couldn't remember what I'd written, but…I **remembered** writing in it. In this library. At this desk.

"Your eye. That blue eye."

I don't know why the words I'd spoken to that girl on the shore of Lake Minazuki suddenly came to mind.

"With that eye of yours, you might be seeing the same things I am…looking in the same direction."

The same things as me?

In the same direction?

What did that mean…?

Several images flashed suddenly before my eyes when I stood up from the chair.

It was something I'd glimpsed the first day I'd **appeared** in this mansion, when I'd come up to the second floor and gone into the bedroom…

First of all—yes—it was on the bedside table.

Now **I could see it** clearly. It was more than an image; I should probably call it a "vision."

A bottle and a glass.

The bottle probably contained whiskey or some kind of alcohol. And—

Beside that was a plastic pill case with an open lid. Several pale capsules had spilled out from inside…And then—

There had been one other thing in the center of the room.

Something white had been dangling from the ceiling, swaying. Oh—it's…

It's a rope.

A white loop had been made at the end of the rope, just big enough for a human head to slip through…

This is…

This looks exactly like…

……

…A voice (…What are you doing?).

Someone's voice (What are you doing…? Teruya?).

I could hear (…Stop it) (…Don't worry about it) several voices.

One was Tsukiho's (You can't…Don't do it!).

One was mine (Don't worry about it…) (It's…too late for me)…

……

……

…My face just before death.

The face reflected in the mirror in the grand entry, stained with blood.

The contorted, stiff features suddenly slackening into an oddly peaceful look, as if freed from pain, fear, and uncertainty…And then.

A faint movement on my lips.

Trembling.

Words were coming out of my mouth. Wringing out my strength on the precipice of death, some words were...What? What could those words have been...?

What was I trying to say?

They were just barely inaudible. Just barely impossible to read. Just on the edge of communicating...Argh—what could I have been trying to say?

Something clattered, and the vision fell away.

I looked over and saw the picture frame had fallen onto the floor. Had I knocked it over without noticing?

I tried to pick it up and return it to the desk. Just then—

I saw the back cover of the frame had come off. The fastener holding it seemed to have loosened with the impact of the fall, which knocked it free.

That was when I noticed something. There was a scrap of paper between the photo and the back cover of the frame.

What is this? I wondered, taking the paper in my fingertips.

On the scrap of note paper, much smaller than the photo, was handwriting. Written vertically in black ink, it was a list of names—five last names.

The one farthest to the right said "Sakaki," and I understood immediately.

This was a note listing the last names of the five people in the photo, written in the order they appeared in the photo. I had made a note of it.

I saw the name "Arai," with the characters for *new residence*, farthest to the left.

Ah, this was it.

So it hadn't been *new well* or *rough-hewn well*, but rather *new residence*. Just as I had imagined before, the boy in the Hawaiian shirt all the way to the left was Arai.

My eyes ran over the other three names, too.

I saw that the two girls were, from right to left, "Yagisawa" and "Higuchi," and the other boy was "Mitarai"...However.

In the next moment—really, almost instantaneously, I couldn't help but notice it, compelled to it. I noticed and couldn't help but goggle.

A slight distance below the names, in slightly faint ink, I saw an "X."

There were two of them.

One was below "Yagisawa." The other was below "Arai." And—

Below each of the Xs, small words explained the meaning of the symbol.

"Dead."

Sketch 4

What does it mean to be in love?

Why are you asking me that out of the blue?

Does it mean you like someone?

Mmm. That you like someone a whole lot maybe. Men usually love women, and women usually love men. Though I guess there are exceptions to that.

Exceptions…So a man could like a man a whole lot, and that would be love?

Well, sure.

Have you ever done that?

Wha—? No, I'm not into stuff like that…

I mean have you ever been in love?

Oh, I see…I'm not sure.

Do you fall in love when you become a grown-up?

You can be in love even if you're not a grown-up. Some kids get right to it.

Hmmm…So, have you? Ever been in love? Who was your first love?

……

You didn't have one?

No…I suppose I did.

What does it feel like to be in love? Is it fun? Does it hurt?

It's...Oh, I don't know. I'm not sure I'm qualified to answer these questions.
Why not?
...Because I can't remember.
......
I can't really remember. That's why...

I

There are things called "crow days."

Several crows, maybe dozens of crows, which you typically don't see very many of around here, gather around a house. They perch on the roof or trees in the yard, occasionally cawing, one after another. The number of other wild birds and birdcalls drops dramatically, maybe because they're afraid.

There are a few days like that each month, and I've always called them crow days.

Why do they all get together on those days? Maybe there's some reason or something sets it off, but I don't really know.

Crows have an image as a sinister bird, but I most definitely do not hate these crows.

They scavenge in trash bags in the city, so I guess they cause problems, but crows are living creatures, so if they know there's food in there, of course they're going to go after it. I've also heard that they fly after kids in parks and stuff and peck at their heads, but they don't do anything like that here. They just caw noisily, and I don't particularly hate them for that.

Actually—

I took care of an injured crow once, a long time ago.

I treated its wounds as best I could, then put it in a cardboard box with a blanket in it and put that in the garage...I meant to look after it until it got better, but unfortunately it died pretty fast. Before there had been any time to tame it or even give it a name.

I buried it in a corner of the backyard. I made a tiny grave marker for it from a scrap of wood.

I made the marker, a misshapen cross. It's still there.

Actually...

After the incident with the crow, I tried several times to keep animals as pets at this mansion.

Not dogs or cats, but lizards or frogs I caught in the yard or insects like praying mantises or crickets...The only mammal I ever had was a hamster. I also received a pair of finches that I tried keeping as pets.

At one point, with the finches, I remember I couldn't stand keeping them locked up in the birdcage anymore, so I let them out. None of the other animals had very long lifespans, and they all died.

I buried them all in a line next to the grave marker I had first put up for the crow. Making the same tiny marker every time I buried one.

Thinking back on it, I wonder if I was doing that to see the thing called "death" in a living creature with my own eyes, to touch it and experience it up close...to try and discover what it meant. I suspect that's what it was.

2

It's possible that my own body is now buried in the earth.

Somewhere in the yard of this mansion, for example, just like those creatures I buried. Or maybe somewhere in the surrounding forest...?

With this thought, I carefully scanned the ground on the property. Looking for any signs that the earth had been dug up and
reburied. But I never spotted anything clearly indicative of that...

I can't deny the possibility that I simply overlooked it. But if
the burial spot were somewhere outside the property, it would be
utterly beyond my power to search for it...

(...here)

Out of nowhere, there came a voice. A fragment of a word.

(at least...here)

What was this?
What could it be?

(...in this house)

Surprised, I tried to catch it...But it slipped through the fingers
of my mind and vanished...

(...forget)

Ah...Whose voice was this?
And when?

(everything...that happened tonight)

The answer was just on the cusp of being understandable.
The meaning so close to being visible.

(...you need to forget)

Smothered by a foggy sense of discomfort, my thoughts came
to a stop.

3

Wednesday, July 17.

Sometime after the schools of the world had gone on summer break. On this day, just past noon, I **appeared** at Lakeshore
Manor.

The sky was slightly cloudy and not particularly summery, despite it being the height of the season. The sunlight was blunted, and the wind only lukewarm…Yes—and it was a crow day.

I could tell this from the voices of the group outside. Because it was not just a single cry, but the overlapping, resounding cries of several birds.

Ah, a crow day, I thought and peeked outside from a window in the second-floor library. An eastern-facing window with no curtains.

As I looked over the trees in the yard, as expected, I saw the coal-black forms of the crows perched on the branches. That alone was probably close to ten birds.

There were also several on the roof and eaves of the first floor, directly below the window. I couldn't see them from here, but I was sure there were several more on the second-floor roof, too.

A sky burial—the term came to mind unbidden.

A custom in some country or other, where in order to bury a dead person, the body is exposed in a field and the flesh is picked at by wild birds until only the skeleton is left.

It didn't seem likely, but could it be that my body, its whereabouts still unknown to me, had been left in a field somewhere and become food for the crows…?

Suddenly captive to such unpleasant thoughts, I gazed out the window at the crows for a long while. That was when—

I heard a harsh sound of a different character than the cawing of the crows.

What was that? Where had it come from?

I looked out a different window and saw the source of the sound.

Below a large magnolia tree at the outskirts of the front yard. There was a human figure picking up a bicycle that had fallen over…

Even at a distance, I could see that the person was wearing a

white dress and a straw hat. Exactly like that time last summer we had stood on the shore of Lake Minazuki and talked...
It was—

Mei Misaki?

Was it her?

If so, why? Why had she come here now?

Now that it was summer break, had she come back with her family to their vacation home? That was probably it, but even so...

When she moved away from the righted bicycle, she put a hand to the brim of her hat and looked up in my direction, then started walking toward the front door of the house. I didn't know what she was hoping to do, but she had obviously come to visit me/Teruya Sakaki.

At length—

Downstairs, the doorbell rang.

I was at a loss, but finally went down to the foyer. But there was no way I could answer the doorbell here. Even if I was to respond, she wouldn't be able to hear my "voice," and if I said nothing and opened the door—if the door opened on its own and there were no one inside—she would be terribly surprised.

I moved smoothly up to the door and peered outside through the peephole. But there was no longer anyone there. So she'd given up and gone home...

...Should I chase after her?

The thought came to me on the spur of the moment. But—

What would I do when I caught up to her?

What could I do in my current state?

In the end, I did nothing—could do nothing—and went back to the library on the second floor.

Scanning outside through the window, I didn't see any figures anywhere. The crows were still scattered here and there, and one crow perched right next to the window spread its black wings wide and let out a *Ka-kaaw.*

4

With a vague sigh, I turned to the desk in the library. I sat in the chair and stared at the photo frame on the desk.

The photo of August 3, 1987—eleven years ago. The photo from the last summer of middle school that brought back so many memories...

The four people in the photo besides me were Yagisawa, Higuchi, Mitarai, and then Arai. Yes—they had been my friends in Yomiyama. My classmates in third-year Class 3, I remembered.

That summer eleven years ago, almost as soon as the vacation started, they had come to visit me at this mansion...or rather, had fled here.

Even if they hadn't transferred schools and ceased belonging to third-year Class 3, when they went outside the city of Yomiyama, they could evade the "disasters." That rule had been passed down to us. And so...

Why not come here and be together, at least for summer break?

I had invited them.

And they had come.

We had spent the month until summer break ended at this same Lakeshore Manor. Knowing the situation, my father understood my feelings and had let them stay for that long visit.

As a result—

During summer break, none of them were visited by disasters. Although we heard that some of the people with ties to the class who had stayed in Yomiyama had died in August...

...These are the memories from eleven years ago that I had so far managed to dredge back up.

I took the note out of the frame and set it beside the frame.

Our five names were listed on the paper. Two of them—Yagisawa and Arai—had "X Dead" below them, which presumably meant that the disasters had befallen them sometime after they returned to Yomiyama in September when summer break ended and before graduation.

Of the four who'd gone back to Yomiyama, Yagisawa and Arai had died because of it. I had gotten the information at the time and written it down in this note. No doubt in the desolate mood indicated by the writing.

And yet...

What were those phone calls about?

The *"we went through it all together back in North Yomi"* phone call had been from Arai. "Arai" was this Arai, and he was supposed to have died a long time ago, and yet...And yet, how could it be?

I hadn't gotten any more calls from him since then, so the mystery remained just that, but...

Speaking of mysteries, the mystery of the missing diary in the desk drawer also remained.

Where had *Memories 1998* disappeared to? Had I myself gotten rid of it for some reason? Or had someone taken it away?

Heaving another sigh, I languidly rose from the chair. Just then—

"Mr. Sakaki."

I suddenly heard a person's voice from downstairs.

"Mr. Sakaki, are you here?"

What?

Was this her—Mei Misaki's—voice?

"You are here, aren't you Mr. Sakaki?"

What was she doing inside the house? Hadn't she given up and gone home?

Had she come in through the back entrance? Now that I thought of it, that door was often left unlocked...Was that it?

I should have gone to see what was going on, but for some reason, I was locked in doubt. Actually, it would be more correct to say I was flustered by this unexpected development.

I stood rigid beside the desk, not moving a single step, and held my breath. Despite the fact that I was a ghost and there was no need to do any of this.

After a while—

I started to hear the intermittent slap of footsteps. She had put on slippers and come into the house.

"Mr. Sakaki?"

Every now and then she would call out, her voice drawing gradually closer with the sound of her footsteps.

"I know you're here, Mr. Sakaki."

I could tell she was coming up the stairs. If she had gone so far already, might she come into this library...?

"Mr. Sakaki?"

At last, I heard her voice nearby. Probably right outside the room.

The closed door was pulled open, outward into the hallway. And then—

Mei Misaki came into the room.

5

The desk was just to the left of the door, facing the far wall of the room. At that moment, I was standing in front of it.

A large display shelf rested against the wall facing the door, offset slightly to the right. Just at that moment, a clock above the shelf chimed.

It was something my late father had been fond of: A door below the faceplate opened and a white owl flew out and hooted to tell the hour. It was a battery-powered owl instead of cuckoo clock. The hour it tolled was one o'clock in the afternoon.

Her attention apparently captivated by the clock, Mei Misaki came to a stop as soon as she'd stepped into the room and looked straight ahead at the shelves. She did not turn toward me. Of course she didn't. Because I was a ghost, something living people couldn't see.

"Oh—"

She made a small sound.

"…A doll."

She took a step, then two, toward the window to the right, as viewed from the door. She walked as if entranced by the far shelf facing her.

She had murmured correctly: There was a *doll* in the center of the shelves. A doll of a girl swathed in a black dress, about fifty centimeters tall.

"That's…"

Mei Misaki's voice once again escaped her. She seemed utterly fascinated by the doll for some reason…

The next moment…

Two events occurred almost simultaneously.

The first was that Mei Misaki moved.

With a short exhalation, she removed the eye patch covering her left eye.

The second happened outside the window.

A sudden, powerful gust of wind shook the glass of the eastward window. An instant later came the cawing of the crows outside.

Kaaw! Ka-kaaw! The many voices jumped over one another, then the flapping of many wings added to the cacophony. The crows that had been perching all over the yard leaped into the air as one.

From my position, I could see the shapes of the flock cutting past the window, black wings spread wide. I was sure Mei Misaki had an even clearer view, standing as close to the window as she was. And then—

It happened immediately after these two events.

With a start, Mei Misaki turned around and looked in my direction.

Her gaze turned directly onto the place where I stood before the desk, and she cocked her head curiously. The eye patch she had taken off dangled from her left hand, and it was then that I noticed it had gotten quite dirty with mud or something.

"Why?"

Her lips moved very slightly.

"Why…are you in a place like that?"

She wasn't talking to herself. Her words could only have been **a question posed to someone standing in front of her**, so—

"Huh?" I "said" it reflexively, despite myself. **"Can you really see me?"**

"Yes…I can…," she replied, her right eye narrowing smoothly. There was a cold light in the false blue of her left eye.

"…Why?" I was the one to ask the question this time. "Why can you see me? And you can hear me, too, can't you?"

"Yes…I can…"

"Even though I'm a ghost."

"…A ghost."

Mei Misaki cocked her head again.

"Teruya Sakaki died, and I'm his ghost, but— No one has been able to see me or hear my voice up until now. But you can?"

"He died…"

She tilted her head further to the side and took a step closer to me.

"Mr. Sakaki…you died?"

"Yes, I did," I replied, my "voice" a terrible croak.

"Really?" she asked, and I replied emphatically: "Yes, really!"

"The story seems to be that I've gone on a trip, but…in reality, I died at the beginning of May. In the foyer on the first floor of this house. After that, I became like this. A ghost…"

My existence acknowledged by no one, unable to talk to anyone, of course…passing the time after my death until this moment in an unnatural, unstable, lonely state.

"…I didn't think you could see me. No one can see me in this form. But then, why can you see me? Why can you hear my voice?"

"It's…"

She started to say something, then trailed off and looked hard at me for a long moment.

Then she deliberately lifted her right hand and covered her right eye with her palm. Her left eye, still exposed—the vacant blue iris that should have been blind—she kept turned on me for another long while, never once blinking…

"Your eye. That blue eye."

The words I myself had spoken to her that day last summer cut through my mind.

"You might be seeing the same things I am…"

Why had I said something like that to her that day? The same things as me, the same direction as me…Ah. It was—

What was it? The question repeated itself, and as if in answer, a single word rose within me, accompanied by an eerie, unsettling trembling.

It was—

Death.

6

"How did you die, Mr. Sakaki?"

With a short breath out, Mei lowered the hand covering her right eye.

"You said it happened in the foyer on the first floor, but…was it an accident? Or what?"

"Even I don't really know," I replied honestly. "I remember the scene from *when I died*, but the memories just before and after that aren't clear. I don't even know what happened to my body after I died or where it is now."

"Was there a funeral? A grave?"

"That's what I'm saying…For some reason, a funeral was never held and I was never interred in a grave."

"…"

"So I think that's probably why I'm *like this*. That's why I'm sure…"

A strong wind rattled the glass of the window once again. Looking outside, the sky appeared to threaten bad weather. It might start to rain soon.

I looked back at Mei Misaki's face as she stood opposite me.

Even knowing that I was a ghost, she didn't appear particularly frightened or unsettled and only blinked her right eye as if slightly befuddled. She now removed her hat and pursed her small lips.

After a moment, she opened her mouth to begin: "Umm," and at exactly the same time I spoke up, "More importantly—"

"More importantly…what?"

She deferred, urging me to continue.

"More importantly—" I plunged ahead. "Your left eye."

"Wha—?"

"Does that eye have some sort of special power maybe?"

"Why do you think that?"

"Well—" I replied with my exact thought. "Normal people can't see me or hear me when I talk…And yet, you can. Could that be because of your left eye?"

"Is that what you think?"

"Yeah. Remember, a little while ago, as soon as you took off your eye patch? As soon as you took off the eye patch and exposed your left eye, you noticed I was here—you were able to see me. So..."

"Mmm."

Holding the brim of her hat against her slight chin, she said, "Yes, I suppose that could be true. Does it bother you?"

"Well..."

"Hmm."

She puffed out her right cheek ever so slightly. A faint, dubious smile seemed to creep over her lips. And then she spoke.

"I'm a bit different. Especially this doll's eye. I'm not like normal people...Even if I explained, you wouldn't believe me, though."

"So I was right..."

"*With that eye of yours, you might be seeing the same things I am...*"

...The same things.

Looking in the same direction.

"Why is your eye patch so dirty?"

"Before, I was..."

She pouted her lips, looking uncomfortable. Then suddenly she pointed at the display shelf at the back of the room.

"What's that?" she asked.

"Huh?"

"That doll. It wasn't there when I came last year."

As she spoke, she *crept* closer to the shelf. She brought her face close to the tiny white face of the doll, which wore a black dress.

"There was a doll expo in the town of Soabi at the end of last year..."

Somehow, I managed to drag the memory forth.

"...I liked this one very much, so I bought it."

"I see. It was nice of you to buy it, Mr. Sakaki."

"Oh?"

"Did you know it's one of Kirika's?"

"Kirika?…Oh, that's right."

I remembered now.

"That's your mother's professional name, right? She's shown me some of the ones she has at the vacation house…After that, I found this at the expo and I wanted it very much."

"…Hmm."

She tossed her head in a nod, then turned back to me and dropped her head to the side. "But—

"Mr. Sakaki, you died, right? At the start of May, in that big foyer on the first floor?"

Both her eyes—the slightly narrowed right eye and the blue left eye—were trained on me unwaveringly.

"I probably fell from the second-floor corridor and broke my neck or something," I replied automatically. "I found repairs to a broken spot in the corridor railing. That's why I think I fell from there."

"What about the reasons for your fall?" she asked, but I shook my head languidly.

"That…I can't really remember."

"An amnesiac ghost, huh?"

Underscoring Mei Misaki's words, a strong gust of wind shook the window glass yet again. Low and far away, there was a sound like thunder.

"…I'd like to hear more," she said abruptly, taking two or three steps toward me.

I grew flustered (despite being a ghost!), and a feeble "Huh?" slipped out of me.

"There must be things you remember or that you've recalled. I'd like to hear more about even just those things. Tell me."

"Uh…Uh, right."

I assented nervously, then spilled a torrent of words on her. Every little thing that had happened since I'd died and become a ghost…As if a barrier had been broken.

I think— Yes, I think I must have been very lonely and very sad these three long months.

Interlude

"…That was how I met Mr. Sakaki's ghost this summer. Afterward, that same day, he spent a really long time telling me all the details."

"You had that long of a conversation with a ghost? Face-to-face?"

"Yup. Rain was falling by the time we finished talking…When I was about to leave, he told me I could take the umbrella at his house, but I said no. I don't mind the rain, after all."

"Hmmm. Even so."

"Something bother you about that?"

"Well, of course it does. I just can't believe—that a ghost…"

"You don't believe in ghosts, Sakakibara?"

"Well…"

"Maybe you don't want to believe in them?"

"It's not whether I want to believe in them or not…Oh, but hey, on the class trip, didn't you say…?"

"There are ghosts all over the place in horror novels and movies, no? And tons of stories about people who actually saw or talked to them."

"Well, okay, but…Actually, no. Novels and movies are just works of fiction. And most of the 'true stories' are fakes."

"And yet, the truth is that I did meet **him**."

"Hmmm. You don't really hear about amnesiac ghosts very often, I guess."

"No?"

"In novels and movies, there's the ghost detective genre... But those are made-up stories. In those, the victim of a murder becomes a ghost and tries to find out who killed them or what really happened to them. The movie *Ghost* could, broadly speaking, be put in that category."

"—Never saw it."

"*Ghost* is such a blanket term—there are so many different kinds. And the ones in Japan are really different from the ones in other countries. The classical Japanese ones are all, 'My wrath shall be avenged!' And they don't have feet...Did this guy? This ghost you met?"

"Feet?"

"Yeah."

"He did. Two feet, just like normal. He wasn't floating or anything, either."

"Ghosts also differ in whether or not they can exert a physical influence. Since they're noncorporeal beings, they can't be touched by anything, and they can slip right through doors and walls and go wherever they want. And then they contrast this ghostly image by opening and closing doors or moving chairs and tables at haunted houses. Those are some other tricks ghosts can pull...The stories are supercontradictory, so even though we call all of them ghosts, they all have some particular specialty, I guess you could say. As far as the ghost you met..."

"Is **appearing** once in a while kind of weird?"

"Oh yeah. Now that you mention it, the fact that he's aware of it himself seems kind of weird. The ghost you met can exert a certain amount of physical influence, right?"

"Opening and closing doors or pulling diaries out of drawers is about it...but yeah."

"But he couldn't answer the phone."

"And he couldn't use the computer in his library."

"But he could go into a locked room."

"…That's what he said."

"In any case, what did this guy die of? All this stuff about alcohol and medicine and rope hanging from the ceiling…The stuff he mentioned seems to be hinting at suicide."

"He said the immediate cause was falling from the second-floor corridor and breaking his neck or something like that."

"And that observation, to notice your left eye—it's, I don't know, pretty insightful of him."

"That's true. Insightful and thought provoking."

"When he said your doll's eye was seeing the same things as him and looking in the same direction as him, he had figured out that was *death,* right? In other words, he had been constantly looking at death. He had been entranced by it. Do you think we can interpret it that way? So he…"

"He ended his own life?"

"Or at least he was thinking about it. And then he actually did die."

"…"

"And then there's the question of why his death was covered up. By his older sister Tsukiho and her husband Mr. Hiratsuka."

"…"

"They might have hidden his body somewhere. I wonder if that's what it is. Anyway, Mr. Sakaki's ghost was looking for it, right? Even he doesn't know where it is."

"Yeah. It sounds like he was upset about it for a long time, in his own way."

"That's a weird touch, too. Or at least unusual. Typically, a ghost would know where its body is, and a really common trope is for them to appear so that they can tell someone, 'It's over here, please come find it'…Although that's in fictional stories. Like in that old horror movie classic, *Changeling.*"

"Never heard of it."

"Urk— Oh."

"Still, a bunch of things happened that day that bothered even me."

"Like what?"

"When I went to visit Mr. Sakaki at his Lakeshore Manor, the front door was closed and no one came when I rang the bell...But when I went around to the back entrance, it was open and I could just walk right in."

"That was pretty bold of you."

"I was thinking someone would be there..."

"But when you went up to the library on the second floor, you ran across a ghost, huh?"

"Something like that."

"You saw him as soon as you walked into the room and took your eye patch off, right?"

"—Right."

"So all of a sudden, this thing you hadn't seen just popped up?"

"...Pretty much."

"Did it surprise you?"

"—Yeah."

"I guess that would startle anyone."

"There were a lot of factors."

"Let's see...There are a ton of mysteries, just from what you've told me so far. Mysteries about Mr. Sakaki's death, and what happened to his body of course, and other troubling details..."

"..."

"..."

"..."

"...Well?"

"Hm?"

"Tell the rest of the story."

"—You want to hear it?"

"How can I not hear the rest? Hmmmm...I wonder what it was

like at the time. The story was that Mr. Sakaki had gone on a trip? Were Tsukiho and her husband really hiding the truth?"

"—As it turns out, yes."

"So then…"

"But I'm going to tell the story in order."

"Oh…sure."

"So with everything the way it was…I decided to do something about it."

"Meaning what?"

"I thought, *I need to see if this is true.* The ghost was **appearing** at places he had a connection to in life, not just at Lakeshore Manor, so I thought there was a chance. And I wasn't really thrilled about it, but I asked Kirika and two days later…"

Sketch 5

…Even though people die, they don't become nothingness. That's what I think.

Like their soul still exists even after they die?

Their soul…I suppose so. Though I don't know if that's the right word for it.

So they go to heaven or hell?

I don't know about that, either, but…

…What about ghosts?

Hm?

*Do ghosts **exist**? If a soul stays in the world of the living, does it become a ghost?*

*There's no such thing as ghosts. It's the job of a proper adult to say that…But hmm. I suppose they **might**.*

Hmmm.

*Maybe I just want them to exist. Anyway, even if they do **exist**, I doubt that every single person becomes a ghost…*

I

On that night of May 3, as I lay on the verge of death, the movement of my lips…

What I had seen reflected in the mirror in that moment often rose vividly to mind and nothing could quiet my anxiety.

What had I been trying to say?

What had I said?

My face spattered in blood. The contorted, taut expression slackening suddenly…and then—

At first, my mouth opened slightly, as if in a gasp of surprise. But—I think—it was just open; I wasn't able to say anything.

Then, my lips moved ever so slightly.

The movement was slight and trembling, but this time words came out…I'm sure of it. The sound of the words, my voice, was barely audible…

No matter how hard I try to remember, even now I continue to feel tantalized impatience, the words just on the verge of hearing, just on the verge of seeing, just on the verge of reaching me…Now, finally, it's…

…The first word I'd spoken.

I feel like it was "tsu."

And the second was "ki."

And then my lips moved again. There was no sound to accompany it, but the round shape of my lips—like the vowel *o*…

…Meaning?

The last sounds I spoke that night were "tsu" and "ki."

"Tsu" and "ki"—that could be *tsuki*, the word for moon. And it's true that there was a half-moon in the sky that night. But that didn't seem to be related at all. So then what did it mean?

"Tsu" and "ki" may not have been the entire word I'd been trying to say.

It was only a part of it, not the entire thing. There had actually been **more**, but I hadn't spoken it. That thought led me to…

The round shape of my open mouth—forming the vowel *o*. So I could have been saying "o," "ko," "so," "to," "no," "ho," "mo," "yo," or "ro"…But…

What if I had been saying "ho"?

"Tsu" and "ki" and "ho"—"Tsukiho."

Tsukiho—the name of my sister.

That night, I might have been trying to convey the name Tsukiho. But why would I do that, lying on the verge of death...?

...

...

...With a faint, almost uneasy smile on her face, Tsukiho had said, "You're right, he did. It seems my brother has been off on a solo trip since the spring."

"Where did he go?"

The person asking had been Kirika. She was Mei Misaki's mother, as well as the craftswoman who had made my doll of the young girl in the black dress. She was a few years older than Tsukiho, a woman with majestic features.

"I'm not sure..."

Tsukiho had cocked her head to one side, never losing her smile.

"He's been like that for a long time. He'll just take off without telling a soul where he's going. And he'll be gone for long stretches at a time...I suppose you could call it wanderlust."

"He sounds as if he enjoys his freedom."

"There have been so many times when I thought he had come back for a while, and he'd be off again to some foreign country or other. So you might say that we're used to this sort of thing from him."

No, that's not what happened—that's not true.

I wanted to stamp my foot, listening to them talk.

That's not what happened this time.

I died and turned into a ghost, and I'm **here**...

...It was at the Misakis' vacation home.

In their spacious living room where bright sunlight streamed through lace curtains. The house was built beside the sea, the windows thrown open to let the breeze in, so the sound of the waves outside was constant. There were also the sounds of seagulls or some other seabirds calling.

At Kirika's invitation, Tsukiho had come over with her two children for afternoon tea. I had **appeared** right in the middle of it. As if stepping down into the scene.

There were six people seated around a large table, on which glasses for drinks and snack plates were arranged.

They included Kirika's invited guests Tsukiho, Sou, and Mirei. From the Misaki family, Kirika and Mei. Mr. Misaki—Mei's father—was also there. Apparently he was in the same age range as Tsukiho's husband, Shuji Hiratsuka, but he seemed much younger than Shuji and had a sort of athletic cheerfulness about him.

"We really do appreciate the invitation, but unfortunately my husband had a prior engagement…I do apologize."

Mr. Misaki waved off Tsukiho's explanation. "We're here on vacation, but I'm sure your husband is very busy. I heard that he's in the prefectural assembly now?"

"Yes, that's right. People were just so insistent, and I suppose he'd made up his mind to do it, too."

"He's a man of so many talents, it's only natural people would turn to him. The election was at the beginning of autumn, was it?"

"Yes. Somehow he pulled through."

"It must be very difficult for you, as his wife," Kirika said.

"Oh no, there isn't really anything for me to help with…"

"Actually, we invited you over today at Mei's request."

"Really! Mei wanted me to come over?"

"She suggested it out of the blue, that she wanted to see everyone. And asked us to be sure to include Teruya, too…Isn't that right, Mei?"

With attention now turned on her, Mei Misaki replied with due politeness.

"Yes, it is. Kirika told me so many interesting stories about Lakeshore Manor last year…"

"Oh-ho. Is that what it was?"

This from Mr. Misaki. He smiled, stroking his sparse mustache.

"Yes," Mei answered, again with all due politeness.

"Now that you mention it, you visited the mansion last year, didn't you, Mei?" Tsukiho asked. "I happened to be over at the same time. Along with Sou and Mirei..."

Tsukiho's eyes crinkled suddenly. It looked to me as if she were holding back tears, but the members of the Misaki family seemed not to notice and she quickly pulled herself together.

"I'm very sorry that Teruya couldn't come."

"When do you think Mr. Sakaki will be back?" Mei asked, and Tsukiho once again set her head to one side with a faint smile.

"Who can say? He really is so fickle and unconstrained."

"Um...have you tried reaching him by cell phone or anything?"

"Teruya doesn't have a cell phone. There still isn't much signal out at that house."

"This area seems to be out of cell phone range, according to the telecom companies."

This from Kirika.

"Oh. I see," Mei replied, nodding. Her gaze, which had alternated between Tsukiho and Kirika, now slid off to one side and stopped **on a certain spot**.

A space behind where Mirei and Sou sat beside each other in chairs. Straight at the spot where **I had appeared** this time.

She wasn't wearing her eye patch. I sensed a strange light in the blue iris of her left eye for a moment. So that's what it was. She could see me again today.

2

"But, Mei, what happened? Why are you wearing that bandage?" Tsukiho asked.

I suspected that she wanted to change the subject, but it was true that Mei had a bandage around her right elbow.

"Oh, I was on my bicycle yesterday and just...," Mei answered. "It's not that bad."

"She was practicing," Kirika supplied, amending Mei's response.

"Oh, Mei. Do you not know how to ride a bike?"

"I was thinking it must be embarrassing at this age and offered to get her private lessons, but, well," Mr. Misaki amended further. "Oh, but you know, there's no sense forcing the issue, eh? Everyone has their strengths and weaknesses. Right, Mei?"

Looking toward his daughter, Mr. Misaki laughed loudly. Mei was silent, her face a blank—but she didn't particularly look like she was sulking, either.

"Meiii! Meiii!"

Standing up from her seat, Mirei walked over to Mei.

"Meiii, you wanna play dolls with me?"

"Hm?"

Mei cocked her head quizzically, so Mirei pointed toward the display shelf standing in the room.

"That. Dolls."

"Now now, Mirei," Tsukiho said, reining her daughter in. "Those dolls aren't for playing with. Understand?"

Several dolls, presumably made by Kirika, decorated the shelf. The dolls were of little girls and were small, but each had a delicate beauty about it.

Mirei whined unhappily, and Sou gave her a contemptuous look as he moved over to the sofa by himself. Tsukiho's gaze followed him.

"Sou seems a bit down, don't you think?" Kirika observed.

"Yes...There's been a lot going on, and he's at a difficult age," Tsukiho replied, sounding a little awkward and looking anxiously in Sou's direction. "I got the feeling he didn't want to come along today. But when I said we were having tea at the Misakis' house, he said, 'I'm coming, too!'"

"Maybe it's because Sou is so close to Teruya, so he misses him?" Kirika suggested. Then she twisted around in her chair and called out, "Sou?

"Would you like some more sweets? Maybe some juice?"

Sou shook his head without a word. The next moment, he stood up from his newly taken seat on the sofa and walked toward the display shelf Mirei had been pointing at. He stood in front of it and peered through the glass at the dolls inside.

"Do you like this kind of doll, too, Sou?" Mei Misaki asked, coming to stand beside Sou.

Sou's shoulders jumped, as if he'd been caught off guard for a moment, then he gave a swift nod. "Um, yeah."

"Mr. Sakaki liked dolls, too, right?"

"—Yeah."

"Is that why you like them?"

"—I dunno."

"Which of these dolls do you like?"

"Oh, uh…"

"Meiii! Meiii!"

Mirei came over to her again.

"Mei, let's play. I wanna play with dolls."

"Now now, Mirei," Tsukiho repeated to get her under control. "It isn't nice to pester people."

During this exchange, Sou returned to the sofa by himself. He lowered his gaze, which held a hint of loneliness, and a quiet sigh escaped him…Then finally—

"I don't know," he whispered faintly. "I don't know…anything."

"Sou?"

Calling her son's name, a hint of alarm in her voice, Tsukiho rose from her chair.

"You know better than to start talking that way again…"

"Oh…yes, ma'am."

"Wow, the weather is so nice."

Now it was Mei who spoke. She turned to the windows where the lace curtains rippled in the wind, and favoring her bandaged right elbow, she stretched her entire body **stiffly**.

"I'm going to step outside."

3

The "outside" Mei referred to was the terrace just outside the room—

I felt somehow as if I'd been invited to join her, and though I hesitated somewhat, in the end I followed after her.

From the terrace, Mei had stepped down onto the grass of the yard and was gazing out at the sea. I gradually approached behind her and—

"Mr. Sakaki?" she asked, turning smoothly to look back over her shoulder. The blue iris of her left eye was aimed straight at me.

"Yes. His ghost anyway."

"Is this the first time you've **appeared** since two days ago at Lakeshore Manor?"

"—I suppose so."

"I see."

Mei twisted her body back around and returned her gaze to the sea.

The house was beside the sea, but that doesn't mean there were waves right in front of us. We were located a few minutes' walk from the shore, a short distance away on a slight rise, giving an excellent view.

After a long while, Mei spoke.

"I saw a mirage from here once."

"Wow. When?"

"August last year. The day before we went back to Yomiyama."

"A midsummer's vision, eh?"

"It wasn't anything as amazing as that. There was a ship going along offshore, and it looked like the same ship was floating above it, but upside down."

"That's really unusual to see in the summertime."

"The air close to the water is cooler and the air higher up is warmer, so light is refracted by the temperature difference and looks like a false image…"

"Right. That's a spring-type superior mirage."

I recited this knowledge that came so easily to me.

"The winter type is the opposite, where the air close to the water is warmer and the air higher up is cooler, so you see the false image below the actual object. Which is an inferior mirage. I have photos of both kinds of mirage at my house."

"—I saw. You actually told me this same stuff last year."

"Oh. Did I?"

"By the way—"

Mei Misaki turned to look back at me once again.

"I feel like we didn't talk about why I was at Lakeshore Manor two days ago."

"Oh yes. I suppose that's true…"

Because I had been busy enough talking about my own situation.

"The fact is," Mei said, then closed both her eyes before slowly opening them again. "I wanted to ask you more details about the accident you'd been in when you were younger. Eleven years ago, in 1987, when you were in middle school."

"…"

"You told me the other day that you were in Class 3 at North Yomi through the first semester of your third year in middle school. You said the bus accident that hurt your left leg so badly happened on the class trip…and a lot of people died in it."

"—That's right."

"After that, your mother also died and you moved here from Yomiyama and transferred schools before summer break. So you managed to escape from the disasters."

"Disasters…that's right. All of that is exactly like I told you before."

I nodded dutifully. After returning my nod in the same spirit, Mei started to speak.

"Actually, I—"

I cut her off.

"You're in third-year Class 3 at North Yomi yourself now. Is that it?" I suggested, anticipating where this was going.

I had thought about the possibility when I read the newspaper article about a student's accidental death…"It's not impossible."

Mei nodded silently, seeming to tremble.

I said, "I happened to see something in the paper at the end of May. Yukari Sakuragi, I think it was. The article said she was a third-year at North Yomi who had died at the school and that her mother had died the same day…Then my imagination just started running wild. Including the possibility that you were in the same class…"

Mei nodded, again seeming to tremble.

"Is this an on year?" I asked. "With an extra person slipped into your class…What about the disasters?"

"—They've begun," Mei replied, her voice subdued. "A couple people have already died. Even the head teacher before summer break."

"Oh…"

"…That's why."

"Why what?"

"If you had lived through 1987, I thought I could ask you for information that might, in some small way, be useful…So that's why I went to your house, I guess."

"And then you found out I had already died and become this ghost…I see. Were you surprised? Or disappointed?"

Mei didn't reply, and instead only leaned her head slightly to one side.

Creee! Creee! a bird called out in the sky overhead. Looking up, I saw several seagulls circling low in the sky.

"Even if I had been alive, I don't think I would have been able to give you any useful information."

Her head still cocked to one side, Mei asked, "No?"

"If anything, I think all I could have told you is 'All you can do is run.' Like we did all those years ago."

"Run..."

"Because at least that saved us. And my classmates who came here for refuge over summer break were safe while they were here."

"Those people in the photo?"

"Yes, them."

Yagisawa. Higuchi. Mitarai. Arai. As I answered, the faces of the four people who'd been in the photo with me rose in my mind, one after the other, when—

I heard the sound of some sort of commotion.

A sound quite unlike the various noises that had pervaded the air to that point; a sound that stirred up a powerful, instinctive unease...

...The shrill sound of a siren. Probably a police car. Several of them.

They came closer and closer and finally stopped. On the road running alongside the sea, visible from where we stood.

"I wonder what it is."

In the same moment Mei spoke, I murmured unconsciously, "What could that be? An accident maybe..."

"Hmm. If it had been a car accident, we would have heard a crash or something loud like that. It isn't that far away really."

"Then what...?"

"Maybe someone drowned. They're close to a swimming spot."

As she spoke, Mei stretched to a fuller height and looked down at where the police cars had stopped. Squinting my eyes to focus, I tried to make out what was happening as best I could.

"Oh…look at all the people they have down there. The police are all heading to the shore…"

The sea breeze carried the sound of people's voices. I couldn't make out what they were saying clearly, but the air felt charged with tension.

"Maybe something did happen in the water?"

"Maybe not a crash, but some kind of incident."

Mei turned back to me.

"Maybe there was some kind of scuffle between people on the beach and they had to call the police, or maybe—"

She trailed off suggestively.

"Maybe what?" I prodded.

And after pausing a bit longer, she responded with this:

"Maybe a dead body washed up on the shore or something. It's not totally impossible that's what happened, right?"

"Er…"

The words *dead body* naturally elicited a strong reaction in me.

A body washed up on the beach. A body that, until it washed up, had been floating in the ocean or sunk below the water. It could be—

It—that dead body…was it mine?

The thought made my vision lurch.

…My body.

Had it been tossed into the ocean after I'd died? And only now…

My body over there. Soaking in the water for so long, it would certainly have gotten bloated. The flesh picked at by fish, it would have been reduced to tatters…

"If it's bothering you, I can go find out?" Mei offered, as if seeing through to my turbulent thoughts within. "Though I think the information will come in before too long, even if we don't rush down there."

"Yes...you're right."

I nodded, but I felt too unnerved to stand still and I staggered, as if hypnotized by the distant sight of the spinning lights of the police cars. Just then—

"What's all this noise about?" Mr. Misaki asked as he came out onto the terrace. "Hmm? What are the police doing in a place like that...? I wonder what happened."

It was at that precise moment—

I don't know why, but I could feel my presence fading. If this continued, I would soon be dragged into the "hollow darkness." I would **disappear**, in the opposite sense of how I **appeared**. Such was the sense of foreboding I experienced.

"...I don't think we should talk," Mei Misaki said in a whisper. "I'll see you later, when no one else is around, Mr. Ghost."

4

Afterward, I only barely managed to stay in that place, but with an entirely unprecedented lack of stability. I suppose the word *sporadic* applies best. Over a short span of time, I appeared and nearly disappeared, then actually did disappear before reappearing...repeating over and over.

I don't know what I looked like to the left eye of Mei Misaki.

The commotion of the apparent emergency on the beach went on for a bit, but in the end we never "went to find out" what was going on...We heard the information from Mr. Misaki about twenty minutes later. I don't know how he obtained the information. He seemed to have gone to another room and made a phone call to someone or other, so perhaps he had a connection with the police. Regardless—

When he returned from the other room, Mr. Misaki informed everyone that "it seems they've found someone's corpse on the beach." I had started to disappear yet again, but then he said that. It felt as if his words riveted me to the spot momentarily.

Everyone's reactions were very different.

Kirika murmured, "Oh my," and put a hand to her mouth. Despite her furrowed brow, her face was nevertheless majestic as she turned it to look out the window.

Tsukiho gave tiny cry of "What!" and then bowed her head, looking somewhat agitated. The color seemed to be draining ever so slightly from her face.

Mirei tilted her head to one side, then turned to her mother and asked, "What's a corpse?"

Distracted by this, Tsukiho told her, "Uh…it's nothing," and hugged her daughter close. "You don't need to worry about it, Mirei."

Sou stood up, swaying, from the sofa where he had been sitting away from his mother and little sister. His eyes still as expressionless as ever, he looked around the room and abruptly murmured in a low voice, "…I don't know," then lowered himself back onto on the sofa.

"What did they say about the corpse?"

Mei was the one who had asked this question. Mr. Misaki stroked his mustache with a slightly uncomfortable look, evidently regretting how inappropriate the information was for his audience.

"They said it was a missing couple. They took a boat out from a beach on the other side of Raimizaki and never came back…And I didn't know this, but apparently there's been quite a flap about it the past few days. The body they just found was probably one of the two of them."

"—That's awful."

"They said it was the drowned body of a woman. They still haven't found the man."

"So it was a woman."

"Yes. That's what I was told, at least."

...The drowned body of a woman.

As my presence began once again to gradually fade away, I listened intently to this conversation between the two of them, and I understood.

The drowned body of a woman had washed up on the beach.

A woman... Meaning **it wasn't my body**.

When I realized that, I noticed that I felt relieved. It was a bizarre feeling.

Why should I be relieved?

Why would that make me feel better?

At this very moment, I still didn't know where my body was or what had become of it. I would have to keep looking for it, and yet...Why?

Perhaps I didn't actually want to acknowledge my death. Could thoughts like that still be inside me, after all this time? I doubted it.

It couldn't be that. This was nothing more than a trick of my mind...Or rather, perhaps, something instinctive deriving from sensations experienced when I was alive.

5

When the day's social call broke up, I was again barely holding on to the place, appearing and disappearing, beginning to disappear...going through that cycle.

While I was in this state, Mei Misaki spoke to me, seizing a moment when no one else was nearby.

"I'm thinking of going back to Lakeshore Manor tomorrow."

She presented the information matter-of-factly in a low voice.

"In the afternoon, say around two o'clock."

"Huh?"

Surprised, I equivocated. She fixed her eyes on me and smiled.

"Can we talk some more there?"

"—It doesn't do much good asking me."

It wasn't as if I could say, *Oh yes, I see,* and promise to appear **there**. That was the reality of being a ghost.

"You can't make it tomorrow?"

"Well…it's not really a question of whether or not it's convenient for me."

"Hmmm. I guess I get that."

Mei Misaki pulled a bit of a face, twisting one cheek, but quickly regained her neutrality.

"Well, whatever. I'll still try going."

Then suddenly Mei raised her right hand and covered her right eye with her palm. One end of the bandage wrapped around her elbow came loose and swayed.

"There are a bunch of things I've been thinking about."

"Oh…um."

I was at a loss for how to respond, and she turned her blue eye directly onto me. Then she said: "I think I understand the situation, but…That place was your home, so please put a little effort into **appearing** there. All right, Mr. Ghost?"

Sketch 6

Do some people turn into ghosts when they die, and other people don't?

They say people who die with grudges or regrets in this life become ghosts.

What if something horrible happens to you and you die? Like Oiwa-san?

That's turning into a vengeful spirit and taking revenge on the person who did the horrible thing to you. There are also times when someone dies without being able to tell someone important how they feel about them or when someone doesn't get a proper burial…Anyway, they're all just stories dreamed up by different people.

So if you get rid of all your grudges and regrets, then you stop being a ghost?

It's called attaining Buddhahood. That's how Buddhism thinks of it, anyway.

Is it different in Christianity?

Y'know, I don't know.

Is "death" different for all the different religions?

The true nature of death is only one thing. But yeah, different religions have different ways of dealing with it.

…

Except.

...Except what?

Aside from all this talk about religion and whatever a
ghost is, I...

I

Even though I *wanted* to **appear** at the agreed-upon time and place, that was no guarantee that I would be able to. Of course, that was the reality of being a ghost as I understood it. But in the end, I **appeared** at Lakeshore Manor just past two o'clock in the afternoon the next day, August 1. Whether this was the payoff of actually putting in an effort, as Mei Misaki had told me to do, I don't know.

It was in the backyard of the house that I spotted her.

She had on a black T-shirt with medium-length denim shorts. She wore a lemon-yellow lightweight cardigan over this and a white cap and had a small red backpack slung over her shoulders...At that moment, Mei Misaki stood in one corner of the yard, beside the line of grave markers for all the animals. She was gazing down at the shoddy crosses that had been crafted from scraps of wood, her fingertips touching the narrow sweep of her chin.

"Hey there," I called out to her.

Turning around, her eyes locked onto me. She had left her eye patch off today.

"Mr. Sakaki?" she asked.

"That's right," I replied.

Mei Misaki pursed her lips, though a faint smile tugged at her cheeks. "So you showed up for me after all."

"Yes, well...Somehow I managed."

I moved forward smoothly to stand beside Mei, who returned her gaze to the grave markers.

"Is this the grave of the crow you were telling me about before?"

"Yes." I nodded, looking down at the line of crosses. "The one on the far left is the crow. The rest are other animals."

"Huh."

Mei stepped over to stand before the far left grave marker and stared down at it, then took one step at a time to the right, looking at each of the crosses in turn, some bigger than others, some smaller. She soon reached the last of them on the far right and stopped there.

"It's like *Jeux Interdits*," she murmured.

I could manage no reply, and she glanced over at me.

"It's…a really old French movie?"

"Oh, that…"

I hurriedly searched through my memory, but only portions of it stirred even slightly, **withered**. The feeling was disappointing, frustrating, unbearable.

"So then maybe—" Mei took another step to the right and looked down at the ground. "Your body could be buried here, next in line?"

"What?"

Taken aback, my eyes shot to where she was looking. The ground looked hard, covered in thick vegetation.

There?

Could my body be down there?

No, it couldn't—I changed my mind at once.

"I don't think it could," I answered. "If someone had dug out a hole big enough for a human body and filled it back in, there would still be signs of something like that, wouldn't there? But the ground here doesn't look any different from the rest."

I also suspected that I had already thought of the possibility that I was buried somewhere in the yard and taken a look around.

"That's true. And the ground looks the same everywhere, not just here," Mei said, lifting her eyes. "Let's look somewhere else, then. Will you lead the way, Mr. Ghost?"

2

"When I came here last summer break, you remember I was sketching the building here in this spot? Not knowing it was your house. Sou found me and went to the lakeshore, where you were…"

Mei Misaki walked through the yard in the opposite direction from where the animals' grave markers stood—eastward on a compass—into the shade of trees a fair distance from the house, then stopped.

"I brought the sketch I was working on that day."

She turned back toward me. Then she lowered the bag from her back and pulled a sketchbook out of it. It was octavo sized with a faded olive cover.

"I forgot this at our vacation house last year. And never had a chance to come back and get it. If I hadn't forgotten it, I would only have my new one—for this year—with me. So I guess that was a lucky break."

What was she getting at?

Unable to guess her intentions, I stood there ineffectually.

A clammy breeze blew past us, rustling the leaves over Mei's head. The sunlight dappling the ground through the leaves danced in time, making it look as if the girl herself were flickering subtly as she stood there.

The blue midsummer sky above was unmarred.

Standing outside the shade cast by the trees, the sun beat down mercilessly on me. As if the sun might burn me away as "impure," since by rights I was a creature who had departed the world of the living and wandered the darkness of the underworld. The instant this thought occurred to me—

The bright afternoon scene changed in an instant.

It felt as if I'd suddenly been thrust into a bizarre world flipped like a film negative. I squeezed my eyes shut reflexively and weakly shook my head.

"Look, see?"

I heard Mei's voice. She had opened the sketchbook and was showing it to me, beckoning me into the shade of the trees.

"This drawing. See?"

She had sketched it in pencil. She had drawn the mansion and its surrounding scenery from this vantage point in neat strokes. As well as several tiny windows nearly on a level with the ground…

"Ah. This is quite a good drawing."

I said exactly what I was feeling, but when I spoke, she chuckled.

"Thank you for the compliment, Mr. Ghost."

Then, her voice sharpening slightly, she asked, "Don't you sense anything when you look at this picture?"

"Like what?"

"Compare this drawing with how the building looks from here right now. It's not a photo, so it's not a perfect representation, but even so…"

I took another look at the mansion.

Compared to the drawing, weeds had grown tall in front of the entire building, no doubt because nothing had been tended since spring, giving it a wild look. In some places, the wall of the first floor and the lower windows were hidden in the shadows cast by the tall grasses…

Which is about all that I noticed.

"Those windows on the bottom there, are they skylights for the basement?" Mei asked, pointing.

"Oh yes, they are."

"I'd like to take a look at the basement eventually."

"That's fine," I answered, then shook my head. "But my body isn't in there. I already searched it."

"—I see."

The sketchbook still open in her hands, Mei Misaki stepped out from the shade of the trees. She walked slowly closer to the building, then—

"What's that?" she asked, pointing again. Turning to look back at me, where I still stood under the trees, she said, "That's not in this picture from last year, either."

She was pointing at a spot in front of the right end of the building. There was something half buried in the rampant weeds, some kind of white ornament.

"Oh...you're right."

A somewhat tall object about three feet in height...Looking closer, I saw it was the statue of an angel with both arms spread out, head thrown back and gazing upward.

"I don't think this was here last year. When do you think it was put here?"

All I could offer was a faltering "I'm not sure." I didn't know. I had no memory of it.

It couldn't be— At this point, a slight doubt lifted my head.

I had overlooked it up till now, but was it possible that my body was buried **there**? That the angel was a marker? But—

Together with Mei, we observed the ground around where the statue stood, but just like at the grave markers in the backyard, we couldn't find any signs even hinting that a human body had been buried here in the time since spring.

3

Next, as Mei Misaki requested, we headed to the garage built next to the house. Once inside the dim interior, I felt strangely relieved. Perhaps the midday sunlight really didn't suit ghosts after all.

When Mei walked up to a dirty station wagon and peered into the driver's side window, I told her with a sigh, "I looked inside the car.

"I also looked in the backseat and in the trunk, and there was nothing suspicious about any of it. Of course, I also looked under the car..."

"When was the last time you were in this car?"

She asked the question as if speaking to herself, but I heard her and murmured, "I'm not sure." *I don't know. I can't remember.*

"When you went over to Tsukiho's, did you always use this car?"

This question I could answer: "Yes, I did. It was much too far to walk."

"Did you let Sou ride in it very often?"

"Well..."

I dug sluggishly through my memories, then shook my head.

"Um, no. I hardly ever let anybody ride in it. When I was driving, it didn't matter if it was Sou or Tsukiho..."

...I wonder why.

As soon as I asked the question of myself, I could see the answer.

"To be honest, I don't think I liked being in the car. But I got a driver's license and had a car because it seemed necessary, and I drove around like everyone else."

"But you didn't actually like it?"

"No. Basically, I think it was...yeah, I think I was scared. Very scared. Deep inside, I couldn't help being scared all the time. Just being in the car was scary…So I didn't like having anyone else in my car, either."

"Is that—?"

Taking a step away from the driver's side door, Mei Misaki narrowed her right eye.

"Is that because you would remember the bus accident eleven years ago?"

"Probably." I nodded as I groped for memories like that. "Because it was a terrible accident."

—Because it was a terrible accident.

"I could never forget that tragic scene."

—I could never forget.

"People tried to tell me that was a special kind of 'disaster.' But car accidents happen even when you're not linked to disasters like that."

"…"

"It would be one thing if I were to get in an accident because of my own driving, but when I imagine someone else being in the car with me, I just…"

—If it's just me dying, that's okay.

—If it's just me dying…

"…So."

"So that's why you didn't want to let people ride with you?"

"That's right."

"Hmmm."

Mei turned her back on the car.

"You've always had that limp, right, Mr. Sakaki?"

Again, she spoke as if to herself.

Then she walked around the garage for a little bit, checking the pegboard where the car keys hung and peering at shelves where all kinds of tools, various components, and **junk** with no obvious purpose were arrayed. As I watched her do this, I began to grow a bit annoyed.

"I've already looked in every corner of this place. My body isn't here," I said to hurry Mei up. "Isn't that enough? If you want to look, let's do it somewhere else…"

It was then that a strange noise sounded, *scre-re-reee*.

Scre-re-reee…crash!

I had barely thought, *What is that?* before—

A huge noise shook the darkness of the garage.

I didn't know what was causing it.

Maybe the bag on Mei's back had caught on a tool sticking out from one of the shelves? This thought wasn't related to Mei's movement, but rather to the fact that the shelves were extremely old and unsteady and may have chosen this moment to collapse. In either case—

The source of the noise was that a set of tall shelves up against the wall, along with the many objects arranged on it, had tumbled over.

"Aah!!"

Mei Misaki was trapped under the fallen shelves…

"No…"

I could see her delicate body. Being crushed without the least resistance…

"…This can't be happening."

The huge amount of dust swirling in the air was like a thick fog. My vision was obscured and I couldn't tell what was going on. But soon enough—

The girl's form resolved into visibility.

Mei had been right next to the shelves, but it appeared she had made a very near dodge. She had escaped the danger of being trapped under the shelves, but she had been knocked to the floor by the momentum. And then, into the spot she now occupied—

The impact had caused the shovel, pickax, and other tools that had been propped up beside the shelves to fall in rapid succession. The sound, reverberating continuously, was both destructive and brutal. The dust that had been kicked up enveloped her prone form like a thick fog...

"A-are you okay?" I ran over to her in a panic. But—

She remained prone, unmoving.

Her backpack was caked in dust, obscuring its original color. Her cap had been knocked off and the **point** of the pickax was right next to her head. *God, if that had been even an inch farther over...*, I thought with a shudder—

"Are you okay?!" I shouted at her, wrenching out a grotesquely hoarse voice. "Hey! Mei...!"

I had run over to her, but now that I thought about it, what more could I possibly do? What could a ghost like me accomplish?

Help her get up?

Do first aid?

What could I possibly...Argggh, what should I do?!

I was maddeningly confused and frantic, feeling like I was going crazy. But that didn't matter—

Mei Misaki moved.

She put both hands against the floor, then her knees...and slowly, under her own power, she got up.

"Oh..."

A sound of utmost relief escaped me.

"Are...you okay?"

"—Guess so."

"Are you hurt?"

"I don't think so."

Mei stood and picked up her cap, then brushed the dirt from her clothes. When she saw the bandage around her right elbow had started to unwind, she frowned slightly and removed it entirely, then looked down at the shovel and pickax lying on the floor.

"Ugh. That's pretty unsettling," she muttered with a sigh. "But...well, I guess it's a good thing we're not in Yomiyama."

4

Leaving the garage, again in accordance with Mei Misaki's wishes, we went for a walk to the shore of Lake Minazuki.

"When I met you here last year, Mr. Sakaki—"

Mei stood on the bank. Her face, touched by sadness or anxiety, she turned to the rippling surface of the lake reflecting the brilliant sunlight.

"Something you said to me that day about my left eye...We talked about it recently, but I had also remembered it. It was a memorable conversation."

"Oh...yes."

"Your eye. That blue eye."

Yes. That's what I'd said that day.

"With that eye of yours, you might be seeing the same things I am...looking in the same direction."

"When you said 'the same things' and 'in the same direction,' you were talking about death. Weren't you?"

Mei watched me, then repeated, "Weren't you?"

"Why do you think that?" I asked her in return.

She replied, "Because...**that** is the only thing my doll's eye can see."

"You can see death?"

"The color of it, yeah. So—"

She stopped speaking and raised her right hand slowly. She cupped her palm over her right eye.

"That's why I said what I did that day. That if you were like me, I didn't think that was a very good thing."

That's right. She had said that when we stood here on the shore that day. I had taken it in with a terribly odd feeling. I…

"…Your body."

Mei turned to face the lake.

"It could be in there."

"In the lake?"

The possibility had occurred to me, too, to be honest.

"Why do you think that?"

"Here seemed **more likely**—more appropriate somehow—than the ocean."

"More appropriate?"

"This lake is half-dead, right? So it just seems somehow…right."

On the dead floor of this brackish lake, in which nothing living existed.

"But…that would mean…"

"It might float to the top eventually, or it might not. Do you want to know for sure? Do you want to see if it's there?"

"What…"

"You're a ghost, so we're not talking about anything too hard here. Though the thought of a living person diving down there to look would be kind of daunting."

When she explained, I realized, *Oh, that's what she means*—and yet I didn't move.

In essence, all I needed to do was leave the relic of life that stood here now and take only my consciousness of "myself" (my soul?) below the water.

I didn't have the first idea how I was supposed to do that,

though. I suppose that as a ghost, I was too imprisoned by this relic of life, too bound up with it.

I turned my eyes away from the surface of the lake and shook my head limply. Through my mind flashed—

The voices from that night (What are you doing...? Teruya?) again.

Awakening once again (...Stop it).

As if seeping out into my consciousness (...Don't worry about it).

Yes—this one must be Tsukiho's (You can't...Don't do it!). And in answer came my own voice (Don't worry about it...) (It's...too late for me)...

When I tried to grasp at the meaning in their words, the voices faded away as if fleeing from me. What emerged to take their place was—

My own face reflected in the mirror on the verge of death.

The movement of my trembling lips. And my own faint voice.

Saying "tsu" and "ki."

That was— As I had decided earlier, I must have been trying to say "Tsukiho." Had my strength given out before I could speak the "ho," despite managing to say "tsu" and "ki"? Or perhaps...

Was there another possibility?

Was there no chance I had been trying to say something else?

I tried to think it through, aware that my emotions verged on the frantic.

For example—

Yes, for example, the name of this lake. Lake Minazuki... *Minazuki-ko.*

I had only moved my lips for the first two syllables "mi" and "na," not managing to speak them aloud, and had only said "zu" and "ki." "Zu" could have sounded like "tsu." The last syllable was "ko," which had the same vowel sound as "ho." And that matched the shape my lips had ended in.

Minazuki-ko...Lake Minazuki.

But why would I have needed to say the name of this lake right before I died? No. I guess the theory is wrong.

In which case, it must have been...

"What's wrong?"

The question from Mei Misaki slowly brought me back to my senses.

"Did you just remember something new?"

"Oh...no," I answered, but then all at once...

(...here)

I heard another voice from somewhere. Fragments of words.

(At least...here)

What was this?

I had heard a voice like this before once...

(...in this house)

...Tsukiho?

So this was Tsukiho again. But even given that—

When was it...and what had been going on?

Utterly confused, I had fallen silent. Glancing at me, Mei Misaki said, "Let's go."

"Oh, um...where are we going next?"

"Inside the house," she replied, her tone suggesting she might as well add, "obviously," then turned her back on the lake. "We're going to search the haunted house."

Sketch 7

But aside from all this talk about religion and whatever a ghost is, I...

What?

I...When a person dies, they can connect in some way with everyone. I get that feeling.

Who is "everyone"?

I mean everyone who died before them.

They die and then connect? By going to heaven or hell?

No, that's not what I mean.

...

Do you know about the collective unconscious?

Ummm...what is that?

Some psychologist came up with it, but it's a concept saying that the unconscious in the deepest parts of a person's spirit might be linked in something like a "sea of the unconscious" shared by all peoples.

Wow.

I don't think that's correct in those terms, but...I somehow feel like when people die, they all melt into this "sea" kind of thing. And maybe in there, everyone is connected.

So then, when I die, I'll be able to see my dad there?

You won't see him, you'll connect with him. You'll connect and, how should I put it? Your souls will become one...

I

We went around to the back entrance and entered the house, then headed for the grand entry.

It was the middle of the day, but due to its large size and lack of windows, the whole foyer was dim.

After sweeping her eyes around the room, Mei Misaki took quiet steps up to the mirror that hung on the wall. Tilting her head slightly to one side, she stared at the mirror, then turned around to look at me and asked, "Where did you fall?"

"There."

I pointed at the floor. Not quite six feet in front of the mirror.

"I was lying on my back and turned my face toward the mirror…"

My limbs bent at bizarre angles. My forehead and cheeks covered with the blood streaming from somewhere on my head. A pool of blood gradually spreading over the floor…The horror of that night came vividly back to me.

Mei nodded cursorily and took a deliberate step toward the spot I'd indicated. Then she looked up.

"So around there in the second-floor corridor. Where the railing was broken."

"Right."

"It really is pretty high up. You really could die from that if you weren't lucky." She gave another cursory nod, then continued. "Also—according to the story you told me the other day, you were trying to say something right before you died. Do you remember what it might have been?"

I told her the unadorned facts.

The movements of my own lips that I had seen at the time. My own voice that I had heard at the time. As well as my thoughts from earlier on the shore as to what it might have meant.

"What you said was 'tsu' and 'ki'..." Mei folded her arms gravely. "I think it's a stretch that you were saying 'Lake Minazuki.'"

"...Yeah. In which case, I suppose I was saying 'Tsukiho' after all."

But...why?

"I don't know...," Mei murmured. She looked like she was going to say something else, but then changed her mind and once again transitioned: "Also—that clock over there..." She looked over at the hall clock. "It struck eight thirty, and then you said you heard someone's voice, right? A voice calling your name, saying 'Teruya'?"

Yes. Someone calling my name in a soft cry (...Stop it).

"Do you know whose voice it was?" Mei Misaki asked. "Like, was it Tsukiho's voice?"

"No." I shook my head. "No, I don't think it was her."

"So then..."

On that night three months ago—

The sight of myself in the mirror, edging toward death. Seeing the shape of the "someone" who had spoken reflected in one corner. It was...

"**It was Sou**," I answered. "Sou was at the bottom of the stairs that night...His eyes open wide, staring vacantly. And he said my name, 'Teru...ya'..."

Yes.

That night, it wasn't just Tsukiho who had come to the mansion. Sou was there, too. He must have witnessed my death.

So maybe that was why one of the times I had **appeared** at the Hiratsuka house, I had talked to Sou in my thoughts as he lay on the sofa.

It wasn't just Tsukiho.

Sou—you were there, too, that night...

"Sou's forgotten." Mei seemed almost to be speaking to herself. "Because what he saw and heard here was such a shock."

2

We went up to the second floor.

After checking the railing where it showed signs of repair, Mei said, "I'd like to take a look in the library one more time," and I assented.

My mind flashed back to the scene on the afternoon three days ago when I had unexpectedly encountered her and I rested a hand on my chest. I was arrested by a strange feeling, as if in this body that was no more than a relic of life, the beating of a heart that was itself no more than a relic of life was thudding through my palm. Lost in this sensation, I preceded Mei into the room, then waved her in.

That afternoon three days ago—

It shouldn't have been possible to see me, but she had; it shouldn't have been possible to hear me, but she had. When I understood that she had this power, I was shocked. Utterly shocked and utterly confused...but I think at the same time, I was as happy as anything else. Joy, as if I had been rescued, if only for an instant, from the isolation that seemed likely to continue into eternity...Yes. That was how I had felt. And so—

No doubt that was why I had gone on to tell her everything about myself, without the slightest hesitation. This girl a full ten years younger than me.

Just at that moment, the owl clock above the decorative shelf announced the time. Four in the afternoon.

After sweeping her gaze around the room in the same way she had in the grand entry, Mei Misaki took several quiet steps up to stand before the desk. Her eyes went to the computer on the desk; then, after tilting her head slightly, she reached out to the framed photo.

"A photo that brings back lots of memories, hm?" she murmured, then her eyes fell on the slip of paper resting beside the frame.

"That's you…and Yagisawa, Higuchi, Mitarai, and Arai. And of them, Yagisawa and Arai are dead, right?"

"Yes," I answered solemnly.

Mei looked at me. "And yet you got a phone call from Arai, who's supposed to be dead?"

"Yes…I did."

"That's odd."

Mei put the frame back on the desk and puffed out one of her cheeks.

"Is this Arai person a ghost, too? One of your peers maybe?"

Next, Mei's eyes stopped on the low chest of drawers arranged next to the desk. A handset for a cordless telephone was lying on top of it. It was part of a set with a charging stand.

Without a word, she picked the handset up.

As I was thinking, *What is she doing? Is she going to make a call?* she nodded and made a satisfied noise and put the handset back on its stand.

"So that's what it is."

"—Meaning what?"

Completely ignoring my question, Mei asked me, "You said there are a couple rooms here on the second floor that are locked, right? I'd like to take a look inside them. Since I still have my physical body, do you think I'll be able to?"

"Well…um, sure."

I pointed at the shelf at the back of the room.

"There's a box over there with a couple keys inside. You should be able to open the doors with those."

3

There were two locked rooms. Both were at the very back of the second floor.

After taking a quick look around the other rooms—the bedroom and closet I used, several long unused spare bedrooms, a "hobby room" with audio equipment and cameras in it—I led Mei to those two rooms.

Using one of the keys she'd brought from the box in the library, Mei opened the door.

We could tell at a glance that the first was simply a storage room. Various cabinets and dressers were lined up against the wall, and several large boxes like hope chests were arranged in the remaining space.

"This room…"

Mei cocked her head, so I explained.

"I kept my parents' old things here."

"Your mother's and father's?"

"My mother died eleven years ago. In Yomiyama in 1987 as part of the disasters. When we evacuated from Yomiyama before summer break, my father put her things in this room…"

I told her the story, tracing out my memories of the past, the outlines of which had no lack of indistinct patches.

"After that, we moved to a different house, but my father left this room the way it was. Then, when my father died and I came to live here six years ago, I put his things in here. I thought it would be nice to put them together."

"I see," Mei Misaki responded shortly, her right eye crinkling. "Your mother and father were close, huh, Mr. Sakaki?"

"…"

"You loved them."

She let out a gloomy sigh, then asked, "Your body isn't in here, is it?"

"No." I shook my head limply. "At least, it wasn't. I looked inside the cabinets and the boxes, but I couldn't find my body anywhere."

The next room Mei Misaki unlocked was also a room from the past, in a different sense from the first one.

As soon as we stepped in and saw the interior of the room—

"Oh…"

A voice that could have been surprise or a groan slipped from her mouth.

"…This is—"

I already knew what I would see, but even looking around again, the sight was bizarre in a way.

The room wasn't all that big, but other than the one wall with the windows, every wall was covered in newspaper and magazine clippings or photocopies, photos, large pieces of simili paper covered in handwriting, and more. At the center of the room stood a long, narrow desk on which a jumble of newspapers, magazines, notebooks, and binders rested.

"This…"

Mei stepped gingerly over to a wall and leaned her face in close to one of the clippings hanging there.

"'Violent Death of Middle School Boy at School. A Tragic Accident Amid Preparations for Culture Festival?'…Did this happen at North Yomi? October 1985…So thirteen years ago.

"This one's even older."

She turned her gaze to another article.

"December 1979. 'Christmas Eve Tragedy. Home Destroyed by Fire, One Dead.'…The fire was caused by the candles on a Christmas cake? And it looks like the person who died was a student at North Yomi. In 1979, that might be one of the years that Mr. Chibiki was the head teacher for Class 3."

"Who's that?"

"He's a librarian now, but at the time he taught social studies. You never heard of him?"

"—I don't remember."

"Oh."

"The article about the bus accident in 1987 is over there."

I pointed at where the article hung.

"The other articles are all about past incidents that happened in Yomiyama, too. There are also some from after 1987. The handwritten stuff is a bunch of tables I wrote to summarize each year. I could only get my hands on so much information out here, so I doubt they're complete."

"And the photos? Did you take them?"

"Oh yes. Sometimes I went to the site of the accidents or nearby to see it with my own eyes…That's when I took them."

"Ah…," Mei murmured again, and wrapping her arms around her thin shoulders, she shuddered. After that, she walked along the wall for a while, her eyes running over each item hanging there, but in the end she let out a deep sigh, as if trying to calm herself.

"You collected all of this, Mr. Sakaki?" she said by way of acknowledgment. "You were gathering information and documents about the disasters at North Yomi."

"Something like that, yes," I agreed, but I didn't feel any visceral reaction to it. You could almost say the sensation had withered away. Surely this was an aftereffect of my postmortem memory loss.

"I think I mentioned this before, but I suppose I've been dragging out my experiences in Yomiyama from eleven years ago ever

since. Still, that doesn't mean that I was trying to somehow stop
the disasters that kept happening at North Yomi after that or that
I felt like I should or anything…I'm not sure how to put it. I felt
like it had nothing to do with me anymore, but I still couldn't forget about it, couldn't get it out of my mind…so…"

—I couldn't forget about it, couldn't get it out of my mind…so…

"Like you were trapped by it?"
Mei's words had a sharpness to them. I lowered my gaze.
"Trapped…Maybe that's it."
"By the disaster that befell you eleven years ago. The death you
witnessed back then."

—Trapped…Yes. Maybe that's it.

"Then your focus broadened from there, to the entirety of the
disasters that have been going on at North Yomi since twenty-five
years ago…"

—Yes…That might be it exactly.

"You were trapped the whole time. Still held prisoner."
"—Maybe so."
After a little while, we left this archive of the disasters, but as
we did, Mei Misaki turned her eyes to the wall beside the door
and came to an abrupt stop. There, in black oil-based ink, written
directly on the drab, cream-colored wallpaper—

Who are you?
Who were you?

Unmistakably written in my/Teruya Sakaki's hand.

4

"When you died on the night in question three months ago, on May 3," Mei began as we headed downstairs. "You're sure that Tsukiho was here?"

"Well...Yeah. I was having a conversation with her...I can still sometimes hear our voices. They sounded heated for some reason. I'm positive it's from that night..."

"I wonder why she came to see you."

"I think because it was my birthday."

I voiced the first thought that came to me when asked.

"That day was my birthday...So I figure that she brought Sou and some sort of present over. And then, Sou was with her when..."

The sight of Sou reflected in the mirror...

The boy's voice calling my name, "Teru...ya," calling softly. His face horribly surprised, horribly frightened...his eyes wide and glassy.

"So the two of them came over. Where were you and what were you doing when they came inside the house, Mr. Sakaki? Just what happened there?"

Her tone suggesting she was half speaking to herself, Mei watched for my reaction.

"So you still don't remember?"

"..."

I remained silent, neither nodding nor shaking my head...

(...What are you doing?)
(What are you doing...? Teruya?)
(...Stop it.)

(...Don't worry about it.)
(You can't...Don't do it!)
(Don't worry about it...)
(It's...too late for me.)

I purposefully dredged up the words Tsukiho and I had exchanged that night and tried to grasp the meaning behind them.

Considering it anew in a calm light, there was one thing meaningful about it. That being— But wait.

That was nothing more than a conjecture, a guess. I couldn't manage to get the feedback/realization that "I remember that."

"Is there anything else missing besides that diary?" Mei Misaki asked after alighting in the grand entry.

"I'm not sure..."

I stumbled over my answer, and she fixed her eyes on me.

"Like maybe a camera?

"There were a bunch of cameras in the hobby room on the second floor, but they looked more like a collection of antiques, right?"

"Oh, that could be."

"Last summer, when I met you on the beach, you had a single-lens reflex camera, right? It looked like it got a lot of use, like it was your favorite one. I don't think I saw it up there. And I didn't notice it in the library or any of the other rooms..."

In all honesty, I didn't really know. Because it was an issue I had never really thought about in that way till now.

When I remained unable to answer, Mei cut across the room with a movement that seemed to say, "Fine. Whatever.

"The library's that way?"

She pointed deeper into the house.

"I'd like to take a look...Then the basement after that. Please stick with me a little longer, Mr. Ghost."

5

"…Wow. This is like the school library. You have so many differ-ent books."

As she walked around the towering built-in bookshelves, Mei Misaki now spoke like the fifteen-year-old girl she was, voicing her thoughts with artless innocence.

"My father had a sizable collection to get me started."

"There are lots of hard books here, too. Did you ever feel like just by being in here, you could understand all the world's secrets?"

"I'm not sure," I replied, following along after Mei. "It would be impossible to understand them all. But…yes, I felt something sort of like that now and again."

"Whoaaa."

Mei turned around, and inclining her head slightly to one side, she looked straight at me. For some reason, that flustered me.

"Uh, I mean…Is that weird?"

"Not really," she said, blinking her right eye. Then a faint smile crept over her lips. "I've experienced things like that myself."

After a bit more time, we left the library and—

"This way."

We returned to the grand entry and entered a hallway con-necting to the rear entrance. Despite being the middle of the day, when no lights should have been needed, due to the dimness of the hall, we almost didn't see a dark brown door that stood part-way down the hall.

"Here," I called Mei over. "This is the way down to the basement…"

When I turned the antique-looking knob and opened the door, at first glance it looked like an empty closet, but at the back was a flight of stairs leading down to the basement.

I turned on the lights for Mei and took the lead to descend the stairs. Still limping slightly on my left leg, the relic of life.

There was another door at the bottom of the stairs, which opened onto a short hallway. The floor, walls, and ceiling were all coated with hard gray mortar, giving the space a rather bleak appearance.

Two doors stood slightly apart from each other on one side. A jumble of old furniture was heaped at the end of the hall.

"It looks like you'd stopped using this place very often," Mei Misaki said. "It's cold, and there's so much dust…"

She pulled a handkerchief out of a pocket in her shorts and held it to her nose and mouth. She put her cap back on her head, pulled it low over her eyes.

Then we opened each of the two doors in turn and looked inside.

"This looks like a storage spot for total **junk**."

The room before us was just that.

Light from outside streamed in through a row of skylights opened in the back wall near the ceiling, so the room was dimly lit even without turning on any lights. Just as I had said, the floor was littered with the very definition of junk…dirty buckets, a **washtub**, a hose, scrap lumber, bits of rope, and for some reason pebbles and bricks.

Mei only peered in from the hall and didn't venture into the room.

"Your body wasn't here, either, right?"

Once that was confirmed, we left the door to the room open.

"What about this other room?"

"Probably about the same, I'd guess," I replied and opened the second door.

Like the room beside it, it was dimly lit thanks to the light outside streaming in. But unlike the room next door, I could see evidence on the line of skylights near the ceiling that this room had once been used for **a specific purpose**.

There was a curtain rod above the windows.

And heavy black curtains at both ends of the rod.

"A dark room…," Mei whispered. "Did you develop photos in here?"

"A long time ago," I answered and stepped forward. "Photography was a hobby I inherited from my father originally. My father turned this basement into a darkroom a long time ago, and he would develop and print his own film…"

"Did you use it, too, after your father died?" Mei asked, moving into the room.

"Only for a little while right after I first moved into the house," I answered. "At the time, I was still taking mostly monochromatic photos. So I developed them here. But I moved on to taking color photos exclusively."

"So you didn't develop color photos yourself?"

"Monochrome and color are totally different, and I didn't have any idea what I was doing."

"Oh, I didn't know that."

"So this darkroom has been abandoned ever since then."

"…I see"

There was a large table covered in dust in the very center of the room, a box-shaped safelight…as well as a lot of other development equipment and tools I had once used that had been left uncared for. Actually, this room felt like more of **an abandoned ruin** than the storage room next door.

"Of course, I searched every corner of this room, too," I said with a sigh. "But my body isn't here. I couldn't find it."

"…Ah." Mei nodded, then walked around the room for a bit before finally looking up at the skylights with the blackout shades once more and crossing her arms. "So we have that other room, and this former darkroom…Hmmm."

Unfolding her arms, she cast a glance back at me.

"There isn't, say…a floor plan of this mansion, is there?"

"I don't think so."

I dipped my head to the side, my face serious.

"At least, I've never seen one."

6

When we left the second room and came back into the hallway, Mei peeked once more into the room next door, and this time went in and picked her way around the **junk**. When she finally came back out, she crossed her arms again and held her head cocked to one side in silence for a bit.

At this point, I, too, had begun to feel, tickling at the edges of my brain, that something somewhere was off. But after a little while, Mei said, "Well, let's go," and turned on her heel back toward the stairs.

"There's nothing more we can do here, anyway...," I heard her murmur, but I didn't follow her meaning—

We went back to the grand entry.

It was already past five thirty. The sun would be setting soon.

7

"I have to head home soon," Mei Misaki had said, but I held her back for a few more moments.

"Listen. I'm going to ask you something kind of strange."

Once we had returned to the grand entry, standing beside the hall clock that had stopped at 6:06...I looked at her.

"Have you ever been in love?"

"Wha—?"

Caught off guard, Mei blinked both her differently colored eyes. "Love? You mean…"

I suppose it would be surprising to be asked something like that out of the blue. I was surprised, too, and I was the one who had asked the question…Or rather, I was terribly perplexed. Even I didn't have a clear idea of why I had asked a question like that.

"…You know, I'm not sure. Ummm." Mei Misaki cocked her head quite introspectively.

"Er…well." I was a bit flustered, but while I failed to find the words to smooth the situation over, a different question occurred to me, and before I had thought it through, I had given it "voice."

"Do you…want to grow up and be an adult right away? Or would you rather not?"

Mei blinked again, and this time she inclined her head slightly, murmuring, "Mmm…"

Finally—

"Either way, I guess," she answered quietly. "It doesn't really matter what I want, after all, since I'm going to grow up either way. If I live, of course."

"…"

"What about you?"

When she turned the question back on me, I was at a loss for a quick answer.

"Did you want to grow up? Or not?"

"Well…"

—But you know, it isn't that great being grown-up.

"I…"

—I wish I could go back. To being a kid.

"…I wish I could go back to being a kid."

"Huh. Why is that?"

"Oh, I…"

—Because I want to remember it, I suppose.

"So what about love?"

"Huh?"

"Have you ever been in love?"

"Oh, er…Well…"

I floundered about for a response, and Mei Misaki kept her gaze fixed on me, her right eye crinkling coolly.

"No?"

At her prodding, I answered with what rose in my mind. "No, I…I have, I think.

"But…"

—I'm not sure I'm qualified to answer these questions.

"…I can't really remember."

—I can't really remember. That's why…

Her right eye still narrowed, Mei Misaki cocked her head to one side, regarding me curiously.

8

"Say, did you…?"

After a space of a few seconds, I started to speak again, but I realized that Mei's eyes were fixed not on me, but on the telephone stand resting next to the wall. The base unit of the cordless phone was on it.

Mei walked over to stand before the phone. She looked down at the black telephone in silence, then lifted her eyes toward me and asked, "This is the phone you heard Arai's message on, right?"

"Uh, yes," I answered, unable to guess her reason for asking. She nodded, an expression of some sort of acceptance on her face.

"The handset in the library was out of battery power."

"Oh...was it?"

"Yeah. So it wouldn't be able to ring when there's a call..."

An old friend, what's-his-name Arai, who's supposed to be dead. Why, despite that, had I gotten a phone call from a man with that name?

Did she have an idea about this mystery? Before I could ask—

"Here's what I think about the Arai issue."

I tried to pluck one thought from my mind, which was, as always, full of indistinct patches and impossible to grasp in full.

"When a person—" I said. "When a person dies, they can connect in some way with everyone..."

"When they die, they're connected?" Mei Misaki twisted her head in intense interest again, just like before. "Is that true?"

"I get that feeling."

"And...when did you start thinking that?"

"Before I died...A long time before, I think."

"..."

"I really did die and became this ghost...But—I think I've said this before—I really don't think what I am right now is the actual state of death. Not this halfway, unnatural, unstable condition."

"So in any case, that's why you're looking for your missing body. That's what you're getting at, right?"

"Right. And then...If I find my body and Teruya Sakaki is

properly mourned and recognized as deceased, then I'll finally be able to **die right**. I'll go to my rightful death. That's how I feel."

"Hmm. I get the feeling we'll find out at least that much somehow."

Mei moved away from the telephone stand and also put some distance between us as she stood in the center of the grand entry.

Just then, in the sunset light that had dimmed the space considerably, the figure of the girl looked somehow like a "gray shade," lacking a physical body just as I did.

"When a person dies, they can connect in some way with everyone," I repeated.

"Who is 'everyone'?" Mei asked.

"I mean everyone who died before them," I replied.

"When a person dies, they melt into something like a sea of the unconscious shared by all peoples. And maybe in there, everyone becomes connected.

"What do you think of that?"

The gray shade didn't move in the slightest, and the girl said nothing in reply. I went on.

"I died three months ago, but since I'm still **like this**, I haven't been able to melt into the sea. Although since I definitely did die, maybe an incomplete link forms sometimes. Namely, that—"

"I see."

Mei glanced back at the telephone stand.

"That call from Arai?"

"Yeah." I nodded. Although I wasn't fully convinced myself yet. "The Arai who called me was indeed someone who had already died. Probably in the disasters eleven years ago. My death formed a link between us since we were both dead, and then…"

"You got a phone call."

"Which didn't sound much like a message from a dead person somehow…But well, that's at least one hypothesis."

"It's a pretty bold hypothesis," Mei Misaki said, folding her arms again, but the girl had transformed back into that shade of gray and I couldn't make out the expression on her face.

9

"I really have to go home now," Mei had said, walking briskly toward the rear entrance. I had chased after her, outside the house.

"Can I see you again tomorrow?"

This is the opposite of yesterday— I thought, as I hesitantly made my request. Mei stopped in her tracks, turned back to look at me, and in that moment, I thought I saw a faint smile cross her lips.

"Tomorrow…I'll meet you here."

It was a mystery even to me why I had suggested it. Did I want to get together with her and conduct a search for the body like we'd done today? Or perhaps…Well, no, the reason didn't matter.

I decided to stop thinking so hard and asked, "You can come?" watching her reaction.

"Hmm…tomorrow…"

Mei pulled her cap down low over her eyes.

"I have some stuff I need to do during the day…I'm not sure. Late afternoon should be fine. Maybe four thirty."

"Oh…okay."

"How about you and your ghost stuff?" she asked teasingly. "Will you **be able to appear** at that time? It won't be too much trouble?"

"Um, well…"

Even if I wanted to **appear** at a set time and place, that wasn't any guarantee that I would be able to do it. But hadn't I managed to **appear** exactly how I wanted to today? So yes, if I made an effort, surely I could do it again tomorrow…

"I'll try and put in some effort."

When I gave this answer, Mei's eye (not her doll's eye) grew a little round.

"Oh," she whispered. "Okay. Well…see you tomorrow at four thirty, then."

"I'll be in the hall like I was today. Go ahead and come in."

"—I will."

With that, Mei spun around.

As I watched the girl walk away under the deep purple of the evening sky, I rested a hand on my chest. I felt the tiny rhythm of that relic of life. For some reason it beat a little wildly, *th-thmp*, as if it would begin racing, but just as quickly it disappeared…The hollow darkness opened its mouth. I was swallowed up helplessly.

Sketch 8

What does it feel like to be in love? Is it fun? Does it hurt?

It's…Oh, I don't know. I'm not sure I'm qualified to answer these questions.

Why not?

…Because I can't remember.

……

I can't really remember. That's why…

…Why not?

……

Why can't you remember something like caring so much about a person?

Caring so much…Yeah, that's definitely true. I remember that. I think I cared…a lot. But…

But what?

*I just can't remember. No matter how hard I try, I can't remember who **that person** was.*

I

And so the next day came: August 2.

Just as I had promised the previous day, I **appeared** at Lakeshore Manor.

I was in the grand entry on the first floor, just as I had said the day before. *I think I'm right on time, too*...I had a visceral sense of it.

I could hardly check the stopped clock in the hall, but listening carefully I heard a *whoo* from the second floor. It was the owl clock in the library. Half past four. I'm pretty sure, that sounds right.

Mei Misaki had not yet arrived.

Just as I had that afternoon of May 17 when I experienced my first awakening after death, I stood before the mirror hanging in the room. The mirror in which, on the verge of death, I had witnessed myself passing away...

...And yet.

As with every other time, my figure was not reflected in the mirror. Even though it faithfully showed everything other than me.

Though I had gotten used to being this way, having it brought to my attention like that made the existence of that girl, Mei Misaki, who could see me in this form, seem all the stranger. How did I appear to her in that blue eye of hers that could see death—the color of it?

Standing before the mirror I remained, waiting for Mei to come. But—

After some time had passed, she still hadn't come.

I waited awhile longer.

Through the silence I heard *whoo* five times in a string from the owl clock. Five P.M.—

What was keeping her?

Perhaps her afternoon plans had gone long and she was running late?

Deciding that standing rooted to the spot accomplished nothing, I started to move away from the mirror. Just then, almost at the same moment—

The scene from the night of May 3, when I died in this spot, flashed into the mirror as I watched. Like a replay video that had been queued up at someone's request...

2

My/Teruya Sakaki's body lying facedown on the deep black floor. A white long-sleeved shirt and black pants. An outfit that made me look somehow like a middle or high school student. Arms and legs splayed out, twisted to bizarre angles. No longer able to move even if I tried.

Head twisted sharply, all the way to the side. Blood fountaining from a crack somewhere in the skull, staining the forehead and cheeks red, a pool of blood spreading slowly over the floor...

...Any moment now.

The bizarrely contorted, rigid face suddenly slackened, giving way to a mysterious, peaceful expression, as if freed from suffering and fear and uncertainty...And then.

The lips moved.

Slightly. Trembling.

"Tsu," "ki"—and then.

I heard a sound from inside the mirror.

The reverberations of a ponderous bell tolling half past eight. And as if superimposed on that sound...

"...Ah!"

A quiet cry.

"Ahh!"

It was Sou's voice. Calling my name.

"...Teru...ya."

Sou's voice. The child's figure captured in a corner of the mirror. The child's face. Terribly shocked.

"Teru...ya?"

Terribly frightened.

"Teruya!"

The child's eyes popping, stunned.

"Teru...ya."

Reflexively, I found myself turning to look at the place where the image of Sou in the mirror showed he ought to have been. At the first steps on the staircase up to the second floor...But of course there was no sign of anyone there now. There was no reason to think there would be.

When I turned my eyes back, the image in the mirror had vanished, but—

All at once, a premonition not unlike fear swelled within me. I hurriedly moved away from the mirror and withdrew to the center of the hall. I then heard—

An alarming noise from above.

Looking up, I saw the railing in the second-floor corridor broken and a person falling headfirst from it...

...Me.

It was me. That was me.

On the night three months ago. Slightly earlier than the scene that had just played out in the mirror.

I turned my eyes away from the unendurable sight of my/ Teruya Sakaki's body crumpled in front of the mirror and looked upward again. A human figure wavered beyond the broken railing. It was—

Tsukiho?

With both her hands planted on the floor, she stuck her head out over the foyer and peered down. In that moment.

"Eee...!" A frail sound slipped out of her. Then, she opened her mouth wide, but no scream followed. All I heard was a strangled sound. I could see her ashen face. I could see the panicked, unfocused movement of her eyes.

"Tsukiho…My sister…"

This…yes, this too was an illusion. Just like what I'd seen in the mirror…An illusory scene projected onto *that*, collecting the fragments of my own memory to reconstruct the events of that night.

—Even knowing that, I couldn't help calling out to her. I couldn't help going up to the hall on the second floor where Tsukiho huddled.

I bolted up the stairs. But I only made it partway up.

I noticed that time was running further back.

"…What are you doing?" I heard Tsukiho's voice saying.

From the hallway on the second floor at the top of the stairs. Those words that had been on the verge of coming back to me so many times, yet whose meaning eluded me. And there—yes—the scene I had been able to imagine or infer, but unable to recall with any sense of reality…

"What are you doing…? Teruya?"

I had just ascended the stairs and run down the hall a ways when I saw two figures before me.

One was Tsukiho.

The other was me/Teruya Sakaki.

The two were moving down the hallway toward me. Tsukiho was following behind Teruya's wobbling, unsteady gait, apparently trying desperately to reason with him…

"Oh…stop it," Tsukiho said, grabbing his arm, but Teruya shook free of her grip and shot back, "Just…don't worry about it."

"Wh-what are you saying?"

"I'd appreciate if you left me alone," Teruya replied roughly, his words suspiciously slurred like his gait. "I want to…"

I want to die—that's what he/I wanted to say. That's why he said not to worry about it, to leave him alone.

"…You don't mean that."

Tsukiho grabbed his arm again. Teruya shook her off.

"I'm done."

"You can't...Don't do it!"

They came into the part of the hall that opened up to the foyer and their struggle grew more heated.

Teruya's steps were more unsteady than ever, but he stubbornly shook off Tsukiho's hands. Even so, Tsukiho chased after him, trying desperately to stop him. A dangerous imbalance was growing in their strength.

"Don't worry about it..."

Teruya tried to shake free of Tsukiho's grip.

"It's...too late for me."

"No!" Tsukiho shouted sharply, resisting.

It was at this point that Teruya's movements and strength, which evidenced a lack of self-control, brought disaster down on him. He flailed and managed to shake Tsukiho off, but the movement was wild and he staggered, falling with his back against the corridor railing standing open to the foyer.

No doubt due to the extreme age of the railing, it was already fragile, and unfortunately, it snapped under the impact. Without so much as a moment to catch his balance, Teruya's body tumbled head over heels and he fell toward the first floor...

...

...This.

This was the truth behind my/Teruya Sakaki's death, apparently. *Well.*

The moment the thought occurred to me, the vision dissipated.

I stumbled slowly down the corridor and checked the state of the railing. It had returned to its **present state** of repair with a new piece of wood patched onto it. When I looked down over the railing, the fallen form of Teruya was nowhere to be seen...

"Teruya."

It was at this point that I heard a voice. It belonged to Tsukiho.

I turned and saw her at the far end of the long corridor. She was standing in front of a door (the one—yes—the one to my bedroom)…

"Teruya, are you in there?" she called out worriedly.

Oh, this is…this wasn't **the continuation of the earlier scene** obviously. Not a continuation, but instead something even earlier than what I had just witnessed…

Time had wound backward again.

Tsukiho had brought Sou with her to visit the mansion and had come up to the second floor looking for Teruya…And she had guessed that he was in his bedroom. No doubt this was the scene immediately after.

"Teruya?" Tsukiho called again and opened the door.

As soon as she had peeked into the room, there was an echoing cry of surprise.

"Oh! What's wrong? What happened?"

I ran down the corridor, following after her figment as she ran into the room. She had left the door open, and I took a somber look around the room. Which revealed—

A white rope hanging from a beam in the ceiling.

A loop had been made at the end of the rope, big enough for a human head to fit through…It was obviously intended **for a person to hang himself.**

A chair had been placed directly beneath the rope. Teruya/I stood upon the chair. He held the loop of the rope in both hands, on the verge of placing it around his own neck…

"Stop it, Teruya!" Tsukiho shouted, running over to her younger brother. "Stop that right now. What are you thinking? Come on, come down from there…"

A powerful smell of alcohol filled the room. Looking around, I saw a bottle and a glass on the bedside table. As well as the plastic bottle I remembered with pills spilling out of it.

The alcohol was whiskey. The pills were probably the sleeping pills I had been using constantly at the time. In a blurred state after taking the two together, Teruya/I had tried to end his own life that night.

Was it fortunate or not that Tsukiho came just at that moment and put a temporary stop to her younger brother's plans, given what would follow…?

"…No, stay out there!" Tsukiho said, turning back to look at the door. "Don't come in here, Sou. I need you to stay downstairs, all right?"

Hearing that, I, too, turned to look at the door. Sou was already gone.

So Sou had come up here, too, following after his mother. But when she asked him to, he had gone back down to the hall on the first floor by himself. And then…

When I returned my gaze to the room, everything had vanished without a trace.

Tsukiho and Teruya. The rope and chair. The whiskey bottle, the glass, and the bottle of pills on the table. Even the smell of alcohol that had filled the room…

The sunlight piercing through a gap in the curtains was extremely faint. Frigid shadows were spreading slowly all over the room, engulfing me as I stood rooted to the spot.

3

It was past six P.M. and Mei Misaki had not appeared. The sun was setting at last, fading from twilight into dusk…

Alone, almost melting away in the prevailing shadows, I lost myself in thought.

*   *   *

If only I were dead...I had often thought this during my life. I had even spoken the words aloud to Tsukiho and Sou.

—If only I were dead, things would be all right.
—If only I were dead...

For example, I rarely let people ride in a car I was driving. Because...as Mei Misaki had pointed out yesterday, cars reminded me of the bus accident eleven years ago. Because that had been such a terrible accident.

—Because it was a terrible accident.

I could never forget that tragic scene...

—I could never forget...

No matter how much attention I paid to driving cautiously, the risk of getting into an accident would never go away. Nor would the risk of a person dying in the accident. So—

I had disliked letting people ride in my car. If by some chance I got into an accident and the person were killed...Just thinking about it was frightening. Very frightening.

Despite being so affected by my experience eleven years ago, I owned a car and drove it around like other people. Giving it some thought, that was probably because I was already constantly thinking, *If only I were dead...*

If only I were dead, things would be all right.

It wasn't just limited to automobiles, either. It was always the same whenever I rode in something, whether a train or an airplane. I was always supremely aware of the risk of an accident or death. But in every case, I wasn't afraid of dying myself. *It doesn't really matter as long as it's just me.* I think that's how I felt.

In other words…that's why.

I had, all that time, been imprisoned by death.

Even as I bore the scars of the past and intensely feared the risk of death, on the flip side I was somehow attracted to it—I think that's what was happening. Over many long years, those thoughts passed through several more stages and transformed into a concrete desire to kill myself…

…That day, three months ago.

That night before my twenty-sixth birthday, at long last I had tried to fulfill that wish.

Using rope, I had tried to hang myself in my bedroom on the second floor. With my mind bludgeoned into a haze by alcohol and pills in order to tamp down the terror when I actually went through with it. But then—

At just that moment, Tsukiho had…

I had just witnessed…No, I had **remembered** the details of what came after.

In the end, it had been an accident.

Tsukiho had been placating me, unsteady as I was with drink and drugs, trying to reason with me, and it had turned into a scuffle, which resulted in…But wait.

Tsukiho might have thought **it was her fault**.

That she had made her younger brother topple from the corridor. That it was the same as committing murder.

Was that why?

Was that why afterward, she had…?

…

…

…

…Afterward.

After my last breath had left me, as I watched myself in the

mirror. After I had been dragged into the hollow "darkness that
follows death," into that perfectly blank space in my memory.
Somehow, it seemed that **I could see** something there…in hazy
outline. It seemed **I could hear** something.

It was…

…

…

…

(…here)

"**Here**…," she had said **that day**.

(At least…here…)

"**At least here…**"

(…In this house…)

"**…In this house…**"

When it reached the point where my body had to be hidden
somewhere in order to cover up my/Teruya Sakaki's death, she—
Tsukiho—had said those things during a discussion with her
husband Shuji Hiratsuka.

So that meant my body had to be…

4

Mei Misaki still hadn't come. Maybe she never would. I—

I suppose I really am alone.

5

The ticklish unease I had felt when Mei Misaki and I had conducted our "search of the haunted house" yesterday. It was…Yes, I had felt it in the basement room we had gone down to search last of all.

What had that sense of apprehension been about?

Questioning myself anew, I realized the truth, albeit dimly. Once it occurred to me, I was astounded that I had never noticed it until now—it was…

That wall at the end of the corridor…

That gray wall in front of which all kinds of old furniture had been stacked haphazardly. **Had that always been that way?**

I groped through my memory, but couldn't feel sure either way.

Was that because the memories had been swallowed up by the "amnesia that follows death"? No, on further reflection, I had hardly ever gone down to that room in the basement during my life, so…perhaps my knowledge of it had always been vague.

I was at a loss as to what to do, but in the end I decided to try going outside first. I had a reason for this.

It was the picture Mei had shown me yesterday. The sketch she had made of the mansion last summer break…

"Don't you sense anything when you look at this picture?" she had asked me yesterday.

"Compare this picture with how the building looks from here right now. It's not a photo, so it's not a perfect representation, but even so…"

Because I remembered that conversation.

Because I remembered she had gone on to ask: *"Those windows on the bottom there, are they skylights for the basement?"*

6

I stood alone in the shade of the same tree as yesterday, in the eastern garden of the house.

I no longer had a good idea of what time it was. The sun had already sunk below the horizon and night had fallen, and Mei Misaki had never come...The wind was blowing. A strong, uncomfortably warm wind.

I couldn't see it from where I stood in the shadow of the building, but it looked like the moon was out. The sky above the roof was faintly glowing. The glittering of the stars peeked out from rents in the flowing stream of clouds.

I took a look at the mansion, as I had done yesterday.

I needed to focus on...Yes, the row of windows at a low spot on the first floor. The line of windows that had been provided as skylights for the basement.

I think Mei Misaki had been trying to point out **the number of windows** yesterday.

The sketch from last year and the building this year had a different number. There were plenty of spots where it was hard to tell due to the overgrown weeds, but when compared closely, **had the number of windows decreased since last year?** Had she had that doubt and suspicion then?

Now that I was aware of it and taking another look...how did it look?

The windows on the left, small and lined up at a height barely above the ground, probably belonged to that room in the basement facing the stairs, the junk storage room. I could make out that much.

Then, the windows to the right belonged to that room that had once been used as a darkroom for developing photos...

What about the windows farther to the right?

Reliant on the faint illumination provided by the moon and stars, I squinted my eyes.

Farther to the right…That would put it up against the right edge of the building. Half buried in the overgrown weeds, I could see something dull white.

That ornament? The statue of the angel. Mei had said, *"I don't think this was here last year."*

Because it was placed right next to the building, I couldn't see past it. It could be a "screen" put there for exactly that purpose.

My only option was to take a closer look.

On the other side of the angel statue—I couldn't find a single window on that part of building below the first floor. The only thing I saw was a blank mortared-over wall…But hold on.

In Mei Misaki's sketch from last year, this angel statue hadn't been here and a window had been drawn on this part of the building. I was sure of it. Which meant—

There had originally been a window **here**, too.

So of course there had been a room on the other side of the window.

A third room built in the basement of the house.

That sense of unease I had felt when we'd gone down to the basement yesterday. If the reason for it had been the way the wall at the far end of the corridor looked…My memory was infuriatingly vague, but maybe the door to the "third room" had been in that wall. It was gone now, and all kinds of old furniture had been piled up in front of the wall, probably as camouflage…

If that were true…

Tsukiho's words that day: *"At least here…" "In this house…"*

According to those words, my corpse had been hidden in the third room in the basement of this house. After it was hidden, the door had been sealed and painted over with mortar, and the line of windows serving as skylights facing the yard had been sealed up in a similar way, leaving them as I now saw them…

This angel statue had been put here to obscure the fact that there were fewer windows, when viewed from the yard. That seemed like a safe bet.

The wind had been growing stronger and stronger.

At the same time, the rustling of the trees and grass had grown more fervent, and the rustling of the entire surrounding forest amplified the sound so that the night began suddenly to show an eerily threatening aspect. The ceaseless noise of insects had stopped, but in its place the cry of a crow rang out, despite nightfall. The area grew abruptly dark, as if the streaming clouds had covered the moon.

I shuddered intensely and pressed both my hands against the spot on the building's wall where the windows seemed to have been painted over.

There was a sealed room on the other side of this wall. And my corpse was hidden inside it. Ah, that's why…

…

…

…

After a while…

With an unexpected shock, I was swallowed up in heavy darkness.

7

…I can't see anything.

Inside a darkness as absolute as the word implies, I felt myself in turmoil. Frightening turmoil.

I can't see anything—but **I feel**.

I feel all sorts of things. All kinds of somehow bizarre…Ah, is **this**—?

In the very midst of my confusion, I barely managed the question.

Where is **this**?

What is this blackness?

A bizarre density, utterly unlike the hollowness of the darkness that follows death. A bizarre oppressiveness. A bizarre prickling and the discomfort that goes with it. A bizarre...

...Truly awful feelings in some indescribable way.

A truly awful sound.

A truly awful smell.

Truly awful...to the point that when I began to notice it, it became almost impossible to bear. Truly awful, like nothing I had ever before experienced...

My turmoil continued. My terrible confusion continued. But—

Somehow, even in the midst of this, I held my ground at the very edge of endurance and once again asked myself:

...*Is **this**...?*

8

This place...Ah, I know where I am. I think I know.

Slowly, slowly, I pulled the answer in.

I died and became a ghost...and I've been looking for my corpse, which had gone missing. I finally realized where my corpse was located. Once I knew that, there was no reason to believe I couldn't go to be with it, as its owner. Even if it's in a sealed room with no entrance...That's why.

That's why I was **here**; it was a natural result.

In the blackness of the basement's sealed third room.

9

...A light.

A light burned in the pitch-darkness.

Light from a bulb dangling from the ceiling. A feeble light flickering unstably.

I cautiously looked around.

There wasn't enough light to be able to see into every nook and cranny, but **this place** was exactly what I'd thought it to be—it seemed certain that I was in a sealed room in the basement.

Dirty walls. Dirty floor and ceiling. All kinds of **junk** scattered about. Quite clearly the look of a room left to ruin…

…

…

…A sound.

Zzzzz…Zzzzzzt…

A high-pitched sound, like something flying around.

Shﬀ…Shﬀshﬀshﬀ…Shﬀshﬀ.

An indistinct sound, like something moving hastily.

The thing flying around…could it be flies? The wingbeat of flies?

When I looked in the direction the sound of rapid movement had come from, I saw several tiny shadows flee into the darkness. The pitch-black, nauseating shadows of insects.

…The unsteady flickering of the lightbulb.

As it flickered, I, too, shut my eyes, as if I might escape the things I had just seen and heard.

10

…A smell.

Something smelled truly awful.

I know something that smells like this. But it was the first time I'd smelled a stink—a fetid stench this intense, to the point of making me retch.

When I closed my eyes, it seemed a hundred times worse.
This almost unbearable stench.
This must be…No. Even that wouldn't be so…

11

Unable to stand it, I opened my eyes and…just then.

I noticed the presence of some sort of large, old apparatus.

It was probably a large, old…boiler or stove of some kind.

Shff…Shffshffshff again.

I heard the awful sound again faintly.

I saw a swarm of black bugs skittering under the boiler or stove or whatever it was. Unconsciously, my throat tightened with a "hurk!"

The lightbulb flickered.

My eyes closed again.

12

…Pain.

I hurt all over.

How could a ghost get hurt? Was this phantom pain arising from a relic of the flesh?

It wasn't a sharp pain, but an unpleasantly throbbing ache pushed into my mind, and once I'd noticed it, there was no blocking it out.

I opened my eyes, and my left hand opened to reveal a small rock I'd been holding for some reason. When had I grabbed that? A completely black stone…Was it a piece of coal or something?

Zzzzz…Zzzzzzt…

The high-pitched sound of wings again, filling my mind.

Zzzzz…Zzzzzzt…

There really were flies circling around inside the room. And not just one—several. Lots. Maybe dozens…

I felt disgusted, irritated, and I blindly hurled the stone in my left hand at them. The sound didn't stop, but instead—

Spluch!

There was a different sound.

Somewhere deeper inside.

Something placed deeper in the room (…*what could it be?*) hit square by the rock I'd thrown.

13

The lightbulb flickered. I had the feeling that each time it flickered on and off, the time it was off was growing longer…

I shut my eyes hard, then opened them again.

In the dim reaches of a shadowy corner of the room, I saw the outline of a bed or sofa or some similar piece of furniture. So that's where the stone had struck.

I drew closer to it warily.

It had a backrest and armrests, so I suppose it was a sofa. A large cloth was draped over the entire thing…Ah, there's a bulge. Yes—a bulge just the size of a person lying beneath it.

…So that's it.
So **the thing** lying there was my corpse.

14

Once again I closed my eyes firmly, then opened them.

When I did, I saw a small rectangular table beside the sofa. I warily drew even closer and realized there were **two objects** on the table.

One was…Was it a camera?

It was the single-lens reflex camera I/Teruya Sakaki had so cherished during life. One of the lost items that Mei Misaki had wondered about yesterday.

The other was also one of the lost items. The daily planner that had vanished from my desk drawer in the library—*Memories 1998*.

This is where it had been?

I picked the planner up and flipped through the pages. I checked whether anything had been written anywhere about May 3—that day three months earlier.

I found it almost at once.

May 3, the very day itself.

The following sentence, in a frantic, sloppy hand:

This is long overdue, but now I can be connected with everyone.

I wish for nothing but this.

15

I stood before the cloth-draped sofa.

That same awful sound. That same awful smell. That same pain all over. Aching, throbbing. Nausea and a suffocating feeling added to by dizziness...I couldn't stop trembling. Trembling in my body. Trembling in my heart.

But...

As the lightbulb flickered out I once again closed my eyes hard, then opened them. Then I told myself:

...It's here.

It's here under this cloth.

The body I'd been searching for.

My body.

16

I reached a trembling hand out to the cloth covering the sofa.

My eyes registered the deep black stains all over the fabric, of blood or something else. No, there was no question. Under this cloth was my...

With trembling fingers, I gripped the edge of the cloth. I tried to fling it back all at once boldly. But my strength failed me—

Flmp. The cloth slid to the floor.

Blrp. There was a disgusting noise.

An overwhelming stench assaulted my nose, and unable to bear it, I pulled my hands from the cloth and pressed them over my mouth...and I saw it.

A corpse.

My corpse.

My lifeless shell, tragically altered.

17

The human shape of it had been preserved, but it was a hideous, nauseating thing that could no longer be called—that I didn't wish to call—human.

Rotted skin.

Rotted flesh.

Rotted organs…

The buttons had fallen off the shirt it wore, exposing the chest. The undergarments were full of holes and even ripped in places. As if ravaged by insects…But no, that was what had really happened. They had been literally devoured by insects or something of the kind. And seeping out, overflowing from below the underclothes—

Rotted skin.

Rotted flesh.

Rotted organs.

I could also make out the tatters that remained of them, clinging to exposed bones.

The strange smell filling the air had, indeed, been the stench of rot coming from the corpse. I understood that dead bodies rot, but human beings are different from things like fish and birds. I had thought it would take more time. That the corpse of a large adult could have turned into this, after being in this place a mere three months at most…

The face was the same.

More than half had peeled away from the skull. There was

almost nothing left of the forehead, nose, or flesh of the lips. The eyeballs were already gone, leaving only the reddish-black eye sockets…And something was moving inside them.

Wriggling and crawling, squirming out, intertwining with one another…

I choked back a moan. "Urk—"

…They were maggots.

So many maggots, crawling out from the eye sockets…Ugh.

They weren't only in the eye sockets. They were coming out of the nose, and the mouth, and from inside the tiny bit of flesh remaining in the cheeks.

The light flickered.

Zzzzz…Zzzzzzt…

The high-pitched whine of the flies' wings filled the room.

Zzzzz…Zzzzzzt…

The light flickered rapidly.

"Whoa!"

Crying out, I shook my head nonsensically. Batting my hands around at random, I tried to shrink away from the scene. But just then—

My feet skidded over the floor and I lost my balance.

Right before it happened, I had a sensation of something being crushed beneath my foot, which was presumably the bugs crawling all over the floor. My foot had slipped on **their** crushed corpses and bodily fluids.

Worse still, I wound up falling forward. Unable to catch myself, twisting around, I fell—onto the sofa. Straight at the corpse laid out there.

Rotted skin.

Rotted flesh.

Rotted organs.

All reduced to tatters, they came to the very tip of my nose, choking me with an overpowering stench.

I flung my hands out in front of me, which landed near the body's rib cage. There was a *shlurp* and a nauseating sensation. The force had torn through the webwork undergarments, and the maggots and other vermin that had ravaged the rotting flesh came swarming out…crawling up at me. Up my hands. My arms. My shoulders.

"Aagggh!!" I shouted, desperately flailing my entire body, trying to shake them off. The rotting flesh that had stuck to my hands. The stench of decay that had wrapped itself around me. The wriggling of the disgusting insects.

"…No."

After my bout of screaming, my voice slipped out of me, defeated, in a faint whisper.

"…This is wrong. This…not this."

The light flickered slowly…And then.

Without a sound, it ended in darkness. The bulb had burned out.

"No…"

Once more within the utter darkness I had first entered, I again shook my head nonsensically. I again flailed my hands around at random.

"No. This is wrong. This…"

My voice was wrenched, cracking, from my body. And I gave forth another prolonged cry.

"…Help me!!"

18

"Help me," "help me"…I think I kept on shouting that, over and over again, for quite some time.

Who was I hoping would save me? How? What could anyone do for me? Even I didn't know.

Worn out from my shouting, at last I sank onto the floor. I hugged my knees and lay like that, on my side, curled into a ball—

"...No," I gasped out, fighting back the suffocating sensation, the nausea. "Not this...not this..."

My own body that I had lost track of after dying. My own body that had been hidden away.

If only I could find it, I had thought.

See it with my own eyes, touch it with my own hands...If only I could confirm "my own death" that way and come to accept it. If only I could do that.

I had thought, *Then, for sure I'll be released from this unnatural, unstable situation.* I would take on the form that was proper to death and thereby connect with everyone else...

However...

Maybe that had all been my own ignorant mistake. Maybe I had been mistaken about some fundamental aspect.

Would I go on lingering here, in this darkness, with this horrifying corpse?

Even when the corpse had rotted away completely, its skeleton exposed, and even the bones had finally crumbled away to nothing, I would be here, like this...Never going to heaven or to hell, never to pass into nothingness, let alone melting away in a sea to become connected to everyone, I would instead be like this, for all eternity...

...I thought I was losing my mind.

No, maybe I already had. I...

As I remained curled up in a ball in the darkness, impossible visions rose up before me and died away one after another.

This place—*this of all places*—might actually be hell. Yes, of course. That could be it.

That night three months ago, after I had written that suicide note in my daily planner, I had tried to take my own life. In the end, my death had transmuted into a fall to my death following a struggle with Tsukiho, but that didn't change the fact that my original intent had been "suicide."

Suicide was a deadly sin—as preached in Christianity, for example.

Suicides go to hell.

And so I had gone. Here. To hell.

(...forget)

All of a sudden, someone's voice rose somewhere in my mind, and I became so confused that I thought my brain would rupture. Not knowing what was happening, unable to take the slightest action...

(Everything...that happened tonight)

Who...was this?

(...You need to forget)

Who...were they talking to?

Who...

"...Enough."

My own voice slipped out faintly, without my willing it.

"I don't want to. Please...help me."

My feeble voice, barely audible from moment to moment...I was weeping.

"Somebody...help me."

Boom!

That was when a sudden, momentous sound shook the darkness.

19

Boom!

The noise continued, and I reflexively covered my ears.

The earlier delusion that *This is hell...* was still vivid in my mind.

Boom!

That some chimerical, terrifying **thing** was coming this way. A terrifying evil beast dwelling in hell, coming to inflict even more pain on me...

Boom!...Kroooom!

The sound was coming from behind me.

Shut up in the darkness, I couldn't see anything, but I think it was coming from behind me, from the wall to the room.

Boom!

I uncurled and rose to my hands and knees, turning to look in the direction the sound was coming from. I found myself backing away from it slightly, but I couldn't keep up my energy and sat down on the floor, hugging my knees to my chest.

Boom!...K-krooom!

It sounded like the wall was being pounded from the other side. Was it the hell beast? Or could it be...? No—

It couldn't... Before my thoughts had taken any more shape than that—

B-boooom!

Almost simultaneously with an incredibly violent *boom*, there came a new sound, *crack!* What could that be? Like lumber snapping...

Crack!

The same sound came again. And then...

...A light.

A single ray of light piercing into the darkness.

20

The sound persisted, reverberating intermittently, while at the same time the light streaming into the room gradually increased.

The single ray became two. Then three and four...and eventually they all joined into a single band of light. Into a swath of light.

The wall was crumbling. It was being broken down from the outside through some person's efforts.

At last, the silhouette of whoever it was came into view in the spreading white light.

It had the form not of a beast, but of a person—a human being. A person I recognized...in the form of a young girl of petite build. It was—

It was.

It was...Mei? Mei Misaki?

She was holding something in both hands. Unsteadily, she swung it over her head, then swung it down. When she did—

Boom!

The sound of it striking the wall.

Crack!

The sound of lumber snapping.

Mortar and fragments of wood scattered to the ground. The edges of the hole she had made in the wall crumbled completely and the shaft of light grew even wider...

"...Oof."

I heard her heave a sigh. There was no mistaking it—it was her voice: Mei Misaki's voice. Her rough, ragged breathing, "Huff, huff, huff..." She continued panting for a while, then once she'd regained composure—

"I know you're in there," she called out.

Independent of the white glow of the fluorescent lights illuminating the hallway outside, the beam of a flashlight was aimed in my direction.

"You are in there, aren't you, Mr. Ghost?"

There was a clatter, followed by a hard, heavy noise. Like she had tossed aside the tool she'd used to break down the wall.

A hole big enough to enable a person to pass through had been broken open in the wall, and she climbed through it. But partway through she froze and made a sickened noise.

"Smells awful…Oh."

The light from the flashlight piercing through the darkness fixated on me as I sat huddled on the floor and—

"**I knew it,**" Mei Misaki said. Her face was completely obscured by the light behind her. "I thought I could hear your voice."

"My voice…?"

At my reaction, she nodded.

"Mm-hm. You said, 'Help me.' From the other side of this wall. So…"

Then Mei slowly ran the light of her flashlight over the dark corners of the room. Before long, the movement of the light jerked to a stop.

"…That's awful."

She had found the corpse lying on the sofa.

"That's…"

"…It's mine."

My voice shook as I answered.

"It's my…"

"Let's get out of here," Mei said.

When I failed to respond, she turned her flashlight on me.

"If you'd rather not, I could just leave you here, too. Do you want me to close the wall back up again? You're a ghost, so you ought to be able to leave anyway."

"Oh, I…"

…Yes. She was completely right. I should have been able to and yet.

Mei Misaki then aimed her flashlight at the sofa in the back once again. With its light illuminating the horrifying dead body.

"That's death—" she said, as if to push it away.

I looked not at the body, but at her. I could tell she had covered her right eye with her empty right hand.

"I see the color of death," Mei went on. "Though I don't exactly need to *see* it. This really is terrible…Come on, you shouldn't stay in here. The body isn't going anywhere.

"Right?" she said and reached her right hand out to me. "Hurry up."

Unsure what to think about anything, I rose unsteadily to my feet. And Mei Misaki gripped my left hand in her right.

Her right hand, slightly moist with sweat and a little clammy.

21

Mei pulled me out of the room by my hand.

Through the hole she had broken in the wall at the end of the hall in the basement, just as I had thought.

A dusty pickax lay on the floor outside. This was—

I was sure this was the pickax that had been in the garage. She had used this just now on this wall to…

"Are you okay?" Mei asked. "Can you move?"

"…Yeah."

"Okay, then let's go upstairs," she urged me. "This…isn't a good place."

She led me toward the stairs, turning back once to look at the hole in the wall.

"It's only natural it turned into that when it's been sitting there for three months in this weather. Rotting and eaten by bugs.

Maybe it's even better that it got that bad. Had you pictured what your body would be like?"

I couldn't answer and simply hung my head. I had lost almost all strength to move under my own power.

With Mei still pulling me along by the hand, we climbed the stairs. As we climbed, she spoke in a matter-of-fact tone.

"The power is cut off to the second floor. It looks like a breaker was tripped."

The power...to the second floor?

"That's why the battery was dead on that phone handset in the library...And that computer."

The computer...in the library?

"So of course it didn't turn on when I pushed the power button. Right?"

When we emerged from the stairwell into the first-floor hallway, Mei Misaki continued on toward the grand entry. Only some of the fixtures on the wall were lit, dimly illuminating the foyer. I could hear a strong wind blowing outside.

When we reached the center of the hall, Mei Misaki let out another sigh.

"All right," she murmured. She let go of my hand and, brushing the dirt from her clothes, continued. "You should be good now."

She turned to face me.

"...What?"

"You found the body you were looking for and...Did you manage to remember? Why that body was hidden in a place like that? Or what led to Mr. Sakaki's death that night three months ago?"

"Oh...maybe."

I gave a slight nod, my head still drooping.

"For the most part."

"—Well?" Mei Misaki pressed. "You found the body...and then what happened? Do you feel like you can connect, like you were saying yesterday? With 'everyone' who died before you?"

"Oh…well."

I dissembled and, keeping my head bowed, looked up to read the girl's face. Mei's lips were tightly pursed, and she was staring at me with a calm expression.

"Nobody knows what's going to happen after death until they die. So that's why I think what Mr. Sakaki believed while he was alive was a fantasy."

"A fantasy…"

"See, death is—"

Mei explained it matter-of-factly.

"Death is more endlessly empty and endlessly isolated than that…And well, maybe it's just my own fantasy, but…Come here."

She waved me over, and I moved unthinkingly toward her. It was several steps away from the center of the hall, toward the mirror hanging on the wall.

Mei stood beside me and pointed deliberately at the mirror.

"What do you see over there?"

"Over there…You mean inside the mirror?"

"Yes."

"That's…"

Mei Misaki was reflected in the mirror. My/Teruya Sakaki's image was…not beside her. Of course, there was no reason to think I would appear in the mirror.

"Only you," I answered quietly. "The mirror only shows you."

"I see," Mei replied with a sigh, then went back to brushing dust off her clothes. "But…it's strange. Because **I can see you.**"

"What?!"

"Even in that mirror, I can see you standing beside me."

"Wh-what does that mean?"

My eyes shot to her face in profile to me. Her gaze was still turned straight at the mirror.

"You must be doing that with the power of your doll's eye…"

"Nope." Mei shook her head fractionally. "I don't think it's that."

She slowly lifted her left hand and covered her left eye with her palm.

"Even when I do this—there—**I can see you.**"

"...Meaning what?"

"It has nothing to do with the doll's eye. I can see you reflected in the mirror with this eye alone."

That was...How could it be?

What did that mean? What was she trying to tell me?

I was rendered speechless by my overwhelming confusion. Mei Misaki looked straight at me.

"You still don't understand?" she asked. "You still can't see it?"

"I..."

"You're the ghost of Mr. Sakaki. Who lost his life here three months ago and whose body was hidden in that room in the basement. Tonight you finally realized where the body was and you went into that room to make sure...But you were calling out for help, right? 'Help me,' 'No,' 'This is wrong'...stuff like that."

"Th-that was..."

I pressed my arms against my head. I was sure I would sink to the ground right there if I relaxed for even a moment.

"You're right, that **this is wrong,**" Mei stated crisply. "You were wrong. From the very beginning."

"...But..."

"Look this way."

I obediently turned toward her. This time, Mei had raised her right hand to cover her right eye with her palm and fixed her gaze on me.

"**I don't see the color of death on you,**" she said again crisply. "**I haven't been able to see it ever since I first met you. So...**"

"...That can't be."

I groaned weakly. Mei lowered the hand covering her right eye and turned both her eyes straight on me...and finally said again in a clear tone, "**So you aren't actually dead. You're alive.** You have to realize that for yourself, first of all."

22

*That's ridiculous...*I couldn't help thinking this, even so.

I/Teruya Sakaki had died.

On May 3, three months earlier, things had happened the way I had finally remembered this evening...and I had died. I died. I died and became a ghost, and this whole time I had been like this...

"That can't...You're lying."

"I don't lie."

"You're lying. Teruya Sakaki died. We even found the body. You saw it just now!" I argued, uncomprehending. "I am Teruya Sakaki's ghost, and...I don't show up in mirrors, and no one besides you can see me, and I appear and disappear all over the place..."

"But you are alive."

Her eyes still fixed unwaveringly on me, Mei repeated, "You are alive.

"You are not a ghost. I don't think ghosts exist, actually. Because I at least have never seen one."

What in the world was she saying? It was crazy. I couldn't understand what it meant. Was it possible...could it be that this conversation itself was some fantasy or hallucination I was having? And in reality, I was still in the darkness of that room in the basement? And Mei Misaki had never appeared? And I was having this fantasy...

"...That can't be."

My voice shook even more.

"That can't...What am I? What are you...?"

"You need to wake up for real soon," Mei said, reaching out both hands and resting them on my shoulders. "Poor thing."

...Poor thing?

"Wh-what do you...?"

"You're still just a kid, but look how tall you've grown. You work so hard to act like a grown-up."

...Still...a kid?

"What are you saying...?"

"You aren't Teruya Sakaki."

...Not Teruya Sakaki?

"Look, cut it out and..."

"You aren't Teruya Sakaki or Teruya Sakaki's ghost. You're..."

I'm...

"Cut it out..."

"You're Sou."

...Sou?

"I'm...Sou?"

"You're Sou Hiratsuka. A little boy who just started his sixth year this spring. Still only eleven or twelve years old...But when you saw Mr. Sakaki's death here three months ago, you turned into this...**You convinced yourself that you're Mr. Sakaki's ghost.**"

...Convinced myself?

"That doesn't..."

"All I can do is guess about why something like this might have happened..."

...I'm Sou Hiratsuka?

"That's..."

That's ridiculous—the same thought.

The many times I had **appeared** at the Hiratsuka house and the time I had **appeared** at the Misaki family vacation house...hadn't

Sou been there as himself? Hadn't Tsukiho and Mei and the others talked to him? Hadn't I seen and heard it happen? And yet she was saying this…?

"That story you originally told about watching yourself dying in that mirror here in the hall? That was Sou, watching from over there—"

Mei Misaki pointed at the base of the stairs.

"It's what Sou saw in the mirror from over there. After he started to think of himself as Mr. Sakaki's ghost, Sou redefined the image as 'what Mr. Sakaki himself saw right before he died.' From which we can extrapolate the rest, I think."

"…"

"Even your problems with your memories as Teruya Sakaki."

"…"

"Because you aren't actually Mr. Sakaki. So even if you allow for 'temporary amnesia due to shock,' it's only natural that you wouldn't be able to accurately remember all kinds of things. Meanwhile, the things you've been remembering **as Mr. Sakaki's ghost** are things you once heard Mr. Sakaki tell you or things you observed when the two of you were together."

—Because it was a terrible accident.

I hadn't said that?

—If only I were dead, things would be all right.

I had heard that?

—Trapped…Yes. Maybe that's it.

"For example, last year when I met up with Mr. Sakaki a couple times and we talked…you were always there with him. And you've been remembering the conversations you heard me and Mr. Sakaki have **not as yourself, but as Mr. Sakaki's memories.** I'm sure there are also a lot of things you learned—**and remembered**—by reading the diaries in the library…"

...

...

...

...Even so.

I couldn't believe it.

There was no way to believe a story like that.

I was Teruya Sakaki's ghost, appearing and disappearing now and then in places he had been connected to in life...And since I was a ghost, I could go freely in and out of even locked rooms in this house, and this very night I had been able to get into that sealed room in the basement...

"Like I told you before, the power's been cut to the second floor, so nobody would be able to make the computer work. It's not that you couldn't get it to work because you're a ghost."

Mei Misaki continued matter-of-factly.

"And I think you just convinced yourself that you were able to go in and out of the locked rooms. After all, you knew where the keys were kept. You didn't slide through the doors or walls because you're a ghost, you actually used the keys to get in and out. You just decided not to acknowledge that fact **to fit your story as a ghost**...That's what I think."

...To fit my story as a ghost?

I was at a complete loss for words, but Mei Misaki fixed me with her point-blank stare and went still further.

"And then there's the day I first ran into you here—"

It had been July 29, a Thursday afternoon.

"I'd come here to see Mr. Sakaki that day...But someone had left a bike outside. Under a magnolia tree in the yard."

Oh...that.

"I accidentally ran into it and knocked the bike over. It was hard to pick it back up...and my eye patch got all dirty."

"—I saw that."

"Oh?"

"I saw from the window in the library..."

I got the feeling that for some reason I had interpreted it as the bike she had ridden over on. But when I thought about it...

"That bike belonged to Sou, didn't it?"

At the very least, it wasn't likely to have been her bike.

After all, two days later, I'd heard them talking at the Misaki family vacation house. Saying that **Mei Misaki can't ride a bike**. So...

"You rode it over here, but that **didn't fit your story while you were a ghost**—it was an implausible fact, so you glossed over what it meant and acted like you never saw it."

...Glossed over it, like I never saw it?

"Tonight that bike saved your life."

Mei Misaki spoke with a touch of heat in her voice.

"I came a lot later than I promised I would...and I'm sorry. There were all kinds of annoying things I had to take care of...I wasn't sure what I should do, but I thought I would hurry over here anyway. It was already dark out, so I thought maybe Mr. Ghost had **disappeared** and gone back home, but...I don't know how to put it. I felt like something was off.

"When I got here, I saw a bike. The lights in the house were off, but since I saw the bike, I figured you had to be here. So I was looking around inside the house...and when I went to take a look in the basement, I heard your voice on the other side of that wall..."

"..."

"I tried shouting back at you, but I guess you didn't notice? You weren't exactly in the right frame of mind, huh? Being in that place with that corpse..."

"..."

Since you were in there, I thought there must have been some way in, maybe from outside the house. But I didn't have time to go looking for it and thought breaking down the wall would be faster. After all, there used to be a door there, and it looked like it had been plastered over…It took a lot of work, though. I felt like I needed to help you, not go looking for someone to help…"

"…"

I was still utterly incapable of responding—incapable of believing it all—and a long time passed.

In the intervals between the strong gusts of wind outside, I could very faintly hear the *hoot* of the owl clock in the library. Ah…what time would it be by now?

"So you…"

At last I timidly began to speak.

"…You can really see me with your eye?"

A faint smile touched Mei Misaki's lips.

"This one, yes," she replied.

With her left hand gently covering the doll's eye that held such mysterious power.

23

And fearful, I turned my eyes to the mirror once more.

It showed something I hadn't been able to see when I last looked at it.

Standing beside Mei Misaki—in exactly the spot I was now standing—looking back at me, head cocked to one side…was the figure of a boy, smaller even than Mei. Sou Hiratsuka.

Wearing clothes different from the ones I'd been aware of until now. Not the white, long-sleeved shirt and black pants reminiscent of a middle school student…but rather a yellow, short-sleeved polo shirt and jeans. The clothes, the face, the hair, the arms…all were filthy, caked with dust, soil, and mud. The eyes were bloodshot, and several tracks of dried tears ran down the cheeks. That was—

That was me? Was it me?

That was…

Still looking at the mirror, I tried moving. The boy in the mirror moved the same way.

I tried walking. The boy in the mirror walked the same way. Without his left leg limping unnaturally.

(…forget)

All at once, I heard a voice.

(everything…that happened tonight)

To the side of the boy in the mirror, I saw the indistinct form of Tsukiho. A phantom of Tsukiho with an ashen face, expression hardened and stern.

(…you need to forget)

Oh…I see.

That night, the shock of witnessing Teruya Sakaki's death had put Sou Hiratsuka into such a stupor and had sent him reeling half in a trance. Tsukiho had issued her order to Sou in that state.

To forget everything you saw and heard here tonight.

Nothing happened here tonight, you didn't see anything—she had been planting those suggestions definitely. That's why Sou had…

"…Oh."

I—myself—let out a long, deep sigh as if to expel everything from within my body, then shyly looked into Mei Misaki's face.

She merely nodded to me in silence and made no further attempt at speaking.

I let out another even longer, deeper sigh. I/Teruya Sakaki departed, leaving only "me" behind.

"...Good-bye," a voice said.

My voice, which had until early this spring been a child's alto but had then suddenly become strangely hoarse with the change in my voice (Good-bye...Te-ru-ya).

Outroduction

I

The display room in the basement of "Blue Eyes Empty to All, in the Twilight of Yomi." In the same old gloominess reminiscent of dusk, in one corner of the cellar-like room—

When Mei Misaki had finished telling her story about another Sakaki she met this summer, I took a series of deep breaths.

I thought I had grown accustomed to the air in this basement room, but once the story reached the final stages, a weird sensation had slowly begun to take hold of me. Each word Mei spoke amplified the "emptiness" of the battalions of dolls, and I felt as if I would be sucked into it…

Unquestionably influenced by an impulse to resist this, I gave voice to a comment with an especially flippant tone.

"So your story didn't actually have a real ghost in it after all."

It sounded so blunt…But no, I had dimly detected a hint of **the truth** partway through the story.

Why?

Because of what Mei had said the night of our class trip in August.

That time when, in one of the rooms of the Sakitani Memorial Hall, she had told me the secret of her doll's eye. When she answered my question of whether she had ever seen any ghosts.

"No…Never," she had said.

She had told me "I have no idea" whether ghosts existed. And that "I think, fundamentally, they probably don't."

What Mei's doll's eye showed her was only the color of death.

It was in a different class from seeing spirits and being able to predict deaths and stuff like that…That was my understanding.

"So essentially, it was a kid playacting."

I continued to unintentially phrase things very callously. Analogizing to the Kabuki and classical Japanese dance technique of "puppet miming," where an actor imitates a puppet, an image had come into my mind of the kid doing "grown-up miming" and "ghost miming." But Mei grunted and tilted her head slightly to one side.

"I don't like that much as a summary."

"Huh?…Oh."

"Sure, the truth is that it was a delusion Sou was having, so I understand why you want to say that…But still."

She stopped talking and I saw her narrow her right eye coldly. That rattled me. I sat up straighter and took another deep breath, preparing to meekly guess at what might come after "but still"—

"From his perspective, it must have been a monumentally important issue."

"Yeah." I nodded, showing an earnest face.

"I get that, but…I don't know, it's so complicated and nuanced, I guess. It seems so hard to explain it just right. I wonder what was really going on in Sou's mind."

"…Yeah."

Drawing her lips tight, Mei nodded.

"I managed to get the overall story from him, and I checked what I could of the facts…but still, the stuff beyond that, you know? No matter how thoroughly he wants to explain it, he can't do it justice."

"I wonder if it gets into stuff like split personalities or being possessed or something."

Sou Hiratsuka, so firmly convinced that he was "the ghost of Teruya Sakaki," who when he **appeared** had felt things, thought, and behaved to the utmost as **that**. These were the words and concepts that bubbled to the surface all on their own when I thought about his state of mind. However.

"I don't think it was quite like that."

I had put the thought out there, then immediately wished I could take it back.

Because a flicker of doubt crossed my mind: *Was it really enough just to apply some **trendy** label to this?* Apparently Mei had the same feeling.

"Treating Sou's **behavior** like an 'emotional illness' and getting a specialist to analyze him and fit him into some '-osis' would be so empty, I think. Though I suppose there are plenty of people who would be happy to do it," she said, drawing her lips still tighter.

"Sakakibara, you said a little while ago that it's 'so complicated and nuanced.'"

"Yeah…I did."

"I agree it's nuanced. But what looks complicated is actually just a lot of simple bits of naïveté all coming together and getting tangled up with each other. You could think of it that way."

"What kind of simple things?"

"Let's try listing off some key words."

Mei slowly closed her right eye, then opened it.

"Child. Adult. Death. Ghost. Sadness…And maybe **connected**."

"Er, that's…"

"Each word is simple by itself, right? But they mingle together little by little while holding onto their individual meanings and get distorted…And the end result was Mr. Sakaki's ghost appearing inside Sou."

"Umm…could you explain that?"

"Wouldn't it be crass to go into any more detail?"

With those words, I couldn't tell whether purposely or not, a slightly sadistic smile crept over Mei Misaki's face. "It's not like this is a question on a language arts test…Right?"

I muttered, unsatisfied, and leaned back in the armchair.

"All the same, though—" Mei said, her smile vanishing. "I'll try and straighten out what happened at Lakeshore Manor on May 3, at least. Because I think it's best to leave it at that."

2

She said that Teruya Sakaki must have been living in sorrow for a long time.

The sorrow of losing so many of his friends in the tragedy of '87 eleven years earlier. Then, the sorrow of losing his mother—

Well, enough for him that he and his family fled from Yomiyama in order to escape the disasters, but people he knew in class and had left behind in the city continued to lose their lives to the unrelenting misfortune. There was no question he had also felt guilt that he alone had fled and been spared. That guilt that the passage of years couldn't erase…And still the sorrow.

At some point in the midst of it all, Sakaki had begun to be fascinated by death, even as he feared it.

Perhaps dropping out of college and traveling all over the place had, from his perspective, been similar to caring for the animals and putting a row of grave markers for them in the garden: a ritual to explore the meaning of death.

In the end, his thoughts had settled in a single direction.

It would be much better for him to die, too, rather than to continue living like this, carrying his indelible sorrow. Then, he would be liberated from it. Then, he might be able to connect to everyone who had died before him.

And so he had reached the certainty that it was time. He had forsaken his own life, thinking that there was nothing else he wished for. And then—

Sakaki had decided to go through with it on the night of May 3, which was also his twenty-sixth birthday. He had written some words in *Memories 1998*, reminiscent of a suicide note, and then he had set up a rope to hang himself and taken sleeping pills with alcohol…And at the moment he had thought it was done, unexpectedly Tsukiho had come over with Sou.

It probably made sense for Sou to believe that the subsequent events, of Sakaki having the misfortune to fall from the corridor on the second floor and die, were facts remembered as "the ghost of Teruya Sakaki." Although in reality, they were based on the memories of events Sou himself had witnessed when he followed Tsukiho up to the second floor, which he had reconstructed from the perspective of "Sakaki's ghost."

Witnessing the life slipping out of Sakaki's body, the man he had adored like a father or big brother, the shock had put Sou into a vacant-eyed stupor, from which he had tumbled into an almost insensate trance. Meanwhile, Tsukiho's first response had been to run over to where Sakaki had fallen, where she saw that he had already stopped breathing. The decisions and choices she made at that point determined how things developed.

She had put Sou, still half-senseless, to bed in a decent location and then made a phone call. Before calling an ambulance or the police, she first called her husband Shuji Hiratsuka.

"Something terrible has happened. Something awful…"

Hearing Tsukiho's voice in snatches—Sou would tell Mei that memory later.

"…What?"

Tsukiho's voice sounding surprised.

"But…but that's…"

She was talking to someone on the phone. Probably Shuji. Sou said he guessed it from the way she talked.

"Right...a-all right. I...understand. Just please hurry...All right...Yes, please. I'll be here."

A short while later, Shuji Hiratsuka rushed into the house. He had a doctor's license and confirmed Sakaki's death, and Tsukiho told him the details of what had happened...At this point, Sou's memories became patchier and patchier, more like guesses.

Should they inform the police of what happened or not?

Teruya Sakaki had absolutely intended to kill himself that night, but in the end the one who had caused him to fall was Tsukiho. The reality was that it was an unfortunate accident, but she was afraid that she would be investigated for her role in involuntary manslaughter. And that the police might wrongly suspect her of even worse.

In any event, the fact that a family member—a brother-in-law, from Shuji's perspective—had attempted suicide would be an immense scandal for a distinguished local family like the Hiratsukas that they wouldn't want to be widely known. And when Tsukiho had a connection like that to the event, they wanted even less for it to become public. There was going to be an election in the fall...After talking it over, the two came to a decision.

Namely, the cover-up.

To erase the fact that Teruya Sakaki had died there that night. To say instead that he had gone on a long trip somewhere by himself. He really did have a streak of wanderlust like that, so it wasn't a far-fetched scenario. He had few close friends, so Shuji and Tsukiho were probably also planning to wrap it all up in the end by saying he had disappeared on his trip.

In that case, they would have to dispose of the body. They would have to dump it or hide it somewhere that no third party would find it.

"At least...do it here."

At that point, Sou thought, Tsukiho had probably spoken up. This, too, was a fragment of conversation that Sou had heard in his flickers of awareness and remembered.

"...In this house."

They probably had a lot of options for hiding the body: burying it in the forest or sinking it in the ocean or the lake...But on that one point, she would not budge.

The Lakeshore Manor her deceased father had so loved, and for which Sakaki had also held a fierce attachment, was a special house. Tsukiho knew that well. So even though they were covering up his death to serve their own purposes, she begged that his body be buried there, at the very least.

At least...do it here.

In this house.

Somewhere inside the house—

In the end, Shuji relented to her request. In the future, when the time came that Teruya Sakaki was declared missing and presumed dead, Lakeshore Manor would pass to his natural-born sister, Tsukiho. There would be no problems taking possession of it. Perhaps his decision had been made with that expectation. And then—

The place they selected for hiding the body was that room in the basement that had gone totally unused for so many years that very few people even knew existed.

The two carried the body down there and decided to make the room itself disappear. They likely decided to have Shuji himself do the construction work to seal up the door and outside windows or to make secret arrangements to have it done. Since he also had his hand in construction-related businesses, it wouldn't have been very difficult to arrange...

When they sealed up the body, they brought Sakaki's single-lens reflex camera and set it beside him, which had no doubt been at Tsukiho's behest. One could imagine with the same intention as placing a favorite object of the deceased with them in the coffin...

As for the diary that had been placed with him, that had probably been to hide evidence. They thought it was a bad idea to leave something that could be read as a suicide note lying around to be found in the bedroom or library. In which case, it might have been better to tear it up and throw it out or burn it. But perhaps they hadn't done so in order to use it as "insurance" in the worst-case scenario.

If by some small chance the existence of the disappeared basement room were revealed and the body were to be discovered, the "suicide note" in the diary would be important. It could be powerful evidence to make the excuse that Sakaki's death had originally been suicide. Done with that in mind...

3

"Apparently that room in the basement was originally built as a stove room."

Appending that explanation, Mei glanced at the round tabletop. Her eyes had landed on the sketchbook she had closed and set down there.

"They would light a big coal stove in there, and chimneys to let the smoke out ran to all the important parts of the house to heat the house in the winter. They stopped using that a really long time ago, so after Mr. Sakaki's dad got the house they just ignored that room."

"So that little black rock Sou was holding really was coal?"

Mei nodded. "Yeah. I think it was a piece of coal someone dropped a long, long time ago, and he picked it up while he was groping around in that pitch-dark room."

...But still.

How had Sou Hiratsuka managed to get into that room the night of August 2? The door and outside windows were all sealed up, and there shouldn't have been any gaps big enough for him to get in through.

When I voiced this question, Mei answered casually.

"Purely by luck, apparently."

"By luck?"

"Given what that room was originally used for, there would have been a chute or hole or something for throwing coal in there directly from outside. Like a tunnel slanting down from aboveground into the room."

You could probably imagine it like a trash chute in a building.

"People forgot it even existed a long time ago, and Tsukiho and her husband didn't know about it, either. And nobody noticed it when they did the work to seal up the door and windows. From inside the room, the hole the coal fell out of probably just looked like it was half blocked with **junk** or something anyway."

"And Sou found that?"

"It looks like it really was purely by chance. Sure, he noticed there were fewer skylights to the basement that day, but he couldn't possibly have phased through the wall or anything since he's not a real ghost. So while he was wandering around near there in a stupor, he just happened to find an old iron lid in the ground, and when he opened it up…"

"That's how he got in."

"I don't think he really understood what happened. It probably felt like falling down a hole. He even said he felt an unexpected impact. And he was covered in cuts that he probably got from that…"

On the night of August 2, Mei had rescued Sou from the basement room. Apparently there was a lot of trouble afterward. All I could think was, *I imagine there would be, yeah.*

"I wasn't sure what to do, but obviously I had to call Kirika first.

I gave her a rundown of the situation and asked her to tell my father, too, and then come over as soon as she could."

"What about the Hiratsukas? Weren't they panicking because Sou wasn't there?"

"Apparently they hadn't noticed," Mei replied. Her voice a touch glum. "After the incident in May, when Sou was at home, he started staying in his room. And I don't think Tsukiho knew that Sou had gone out after the sun went down that night."

"Hmm. When you say that, it makes me think of…"

I felt like the isolation Sou experienced in the Hiratsuka house was being shoved into my face. I was sure his home environment had been basically the same even before what happened in May.

"After that, all kinds of stuff happened…In the end, the police came. Sou went to the hospital. And one of the police officers asked me a ton of questions, but…"

There were a lot of questions about how the incident was handled after that. The fact that a body had been discovered in the basement was never announced publicly, and for some reason, neither of the Hiratsukas wound up being arrested for suspicion of illegally disposing of a body or anything else.

The only change was that Shuji Hiratsuka withdrew from the election he had planned to join for the fall. I don't know what grown-up dynamics were at work there. Even when Mei asked Kirika what was going on, she only got fake-sounding answers.

4

How had Sou Hiratsuka become convinced that he was the ghost of Teruya Sakaki?

I know it makes me look crass, but I attempted to work out an explanation for it afterward. I couldn't stop myself. Using the key words Mei pointed out earlier as clues—

"Sou cared a lot about Mr. Sakaki. Because to Sou, Mr. Sakaki played a role more like a father or an older brother…"

†   †

Do you want to grow up? Or would you rather not?

…Whichever.

"Whichever"?

You're not free as a kid…But I hate grown-ups.

You hate them?

It depends on the person. If I could be a grown-up I like, I'd want to grow up right now.

†   †

"On the other hand, Sou hated adults. I imagine he probably disliked most adults who weren't Mr. Sakaki. Including Mr. Hiratsuka, who was Tsukiho's second husband, and Tsukiho who poured all her affection onto little Mirei, her child with Mr. Hiratsuka, and probably the teachers at his school, too…And that's why.

"That's why Sou thought that.

"That if he could be a grown-up he liked, he'd want to grow up right away. In other words, **if he could be like Mr. Sakaki, he would want to grow up as fast as he could**…"

†   †

What happens to people when they die?

—Hmm?

Do they move on to the afterlife when they die?

Well…who can say?

†

Do ghosts exist? If a soul stays in "the world of the living," does it become a ghost?

There's no such thing as ghosts. It's the job of a proper adult to say that…But hmm. I suppose **they might.**

Hmmm.

Maybe I just **want them to exist.**

†   †

"And Mr. Sakaki, who he idolized so much, died right in front of Sou.

"The person he loved most and who was most important to him in that moment. The only adult he wanted to grow up to be… That's who died.

"Sou didn't want to accept the reality that Mr. Sakaki was gone. But the dead didn't come back to life for him.

"Sou had lost the ideal adult he wanted to grow up to be. If he couldn't be like him, he'd rather stay a child, without any freedom. But even if he didn't want to, he would still grow up…"

†   †

Do some people turn into ghosts when they die and other people don't?

They say people who die with grudges or regrets in this life become ghosts.

What if something horrible happens to you and you die? Like Oiwa-san?

That's turning into a vengeful spirit and taking revenge on the person who did the horrible thing to you. There's also when someone dies without being able to tell someone important how they feel about them **or when someone doesn't get a proper burial**...

† †

"Maybe if Tsukiho and her husband had called an ambulance or the police that night. If Mr. Sakaki's death had become public and they had held a proper funeral and burial—

"Then maybe Sou wouldn't have become a 'ghost.'

"But the reality turned out different.

"When Tsukiho ordered Sou to forget what had happened that night and it became subliminal...and combined with the major shock he had undergone, he really did seal away his memories of that night and shut down emotionally. Mr. Sakaki's death was covered up and he couldn't be properly mourned by everyone...And then 'the ghost of Teruya Sakaki' **awoke** inside Sou and started **to appear** occasionally. But from Sou's perspective, that was also linked to granting his own desire under a different guise.

"In one sense, there was his desire for Mr. Sakaki to stay among the living. For him to turn into a ghost and be by Sou's side, even if he was dead.

"In another sense, there was Sou's desire to not become one of the grown-ups he hates, but instead to become the grown-up he likes best of all, as fast as he could. If he was going to turn into a grown-up he hates, then he preferred to stay a kid. But he was going to grow up whether he liked it or not. So given that, he would want to become the 'adult' who was 'the ghost of Teruya

Sakaki, who he liked best.' Maybe he also wanted to, in some sense, stop time for himself by doing that..."

†   †

When a person dies, **they can connect in some way with everyone.** I get that feeling.

Who is "everyone"?

I mean everyone who died before them.

†   †

"The fact that Sou woke up as 'the ghost of Teruya Sakaki' and started to search for Mr. Sakaki's missing body, while occasionally popping up here and there to go through his memories as a 'ghost'...that might have been an act on Mr. Sakaki's behalf.

"Rather than Sou fulfilling his own desires, the 'ghost of Teruya Sakaki' might have kept at it for the sake of his own/Teruya Sakaki's death. If he could find his body and make it public, and get his proper 'death' to take him, then he/Teruya Sakaki would be able to connect with 'everyone.' Mr. Sakaki had always wanted that...And that's why."

5

"What do you think?"

I finished my crass analysis, feeling immensely nervous, and tried to gauge Mei's reaction.

Mei's arms were folded over her chest gravely.

"It's good enough, I suppose," she answered. An image of Mr. Chibiki in a pose I had often seen him adopt seemed to superimpose itself on her. "It's not really an issue where you can point to one right answer…It's just…"

"What?"

"I feel kind of awful making this analogy, but maybe that ghost was kind of like a mirage?"

"A mirage?"

Now that she mentioned it, there had been a quick scene in her story about a mirage you could see in the ocean at Hinami.

"Yes," Mei replied, shutting her right eye. "An illusory scene, appearing and then disappearing. Light gets bent by temperature differences in the air, and the original scene appears in a different place, stretched out or compressed or turned upside down…a twisted, false image."

"Right."

"What everyone around him saw was the true image of the boy Sou Hiratsuka. But what the boy himself saw was like that, a false image of himself twisted like a mirage. That was the 'ghost of Mr. Sakaki.'"

"Yeah…"

"The temperature difference in the air is, in other words, the difference in momentum of the particles in the air. You could also say it's the difference in density per unit time."

"Sure, I guess."

"In Sou's case, the cause of the bending was a difference in temperature in his heart. Or the density of sorrow in his heart. It got to be too much and his true form twisted into that false image… That's what I think."

Mei let out a sigh, and I nodded, thinking it over.

It began to occur to me that, oddly, this analogy fit much more perfectly than my strained, pedantic explanation—

"Speaking of awful," I said. "I thought up a rule."

"A rule?"

"More like a pattern to recognize the 'ghost of Teruya Sakaki.'"

"Oh?"

Mei looked at me with intense interest.

Even as I was seized again by nerves, I tried to describe the problem that I had been thinking about for some time and had tried to summarize in my head.

"While Sou **was appearing** as a ghost, how was Sou himself being perceived? It couldn't possibly have been the same in every situation. So I think it probably broke down into patterns like this…"

Then I showed her the following three "patterns":

1. When he was the only person there. The "ghost of Teruya Sakaki" would perceive the physical form of Sou Hiratsuka as "not there." Therefore, even if he were to look in a mirror, he wouldn't see himself (i.e., Sou).

2. When he was with other people, one or more of whom were acknowledging Sou's presence. In such situations, the ghost would also recognize that Sou was there. The ghost would construct a perspective of a "soul" having an out-of-body experience and would be aware of his own (i.e., Sou's) appearance, words, and actions.

3. Cases where he was with other people, but those people could see the ghost (as understood by the ghost himself). In cases where the ghost was alone with one such person, he would perceive Sou as "not there," just as in case one.

"The only person fitting the third pattern was Mei Misaki," I continued, recalling the minor details of the story she had told me. "For example, when the ghost **appeared** at the afternoon tea at your family's vacation house. You went out onto the terrace by yourself in a way that seemed to be an invitation, and Sou followed you out, right? So then, when the two of you were alone, he started talking to you as the ghost. But then, in that situation, Sou himself became 'not there'…

"And then your father came outside. Since he acted like Sou was there with you, the ghost's perception had to change, too, so he couldn't talk to you directly anymore and started to disappear..."

After a few moments, Mei nodded. "You're right. I think that's how it went."

"And then—" I pressed on. "The part that bothered me most was why would Sou have misunderstood in the first place? About your left eye being able to see him as a ghost? That you could see him?"

I wanted to set this part straight.

Thinking back over Mei's story, the reason for this was still a mystery to me. Because when the two had run into each other for the first time over the summer in the library of Lakeshore Manor, that had struck me as a situation where "as soon as she took the eye patch off her left eye, she was able to see the ghost who had until then been invisible to her."

"That was—" Resting her fingers on the edge of her eye patch, Mei replied in a detached tone, "That was actually helped by chance a little bit, too, to turn out the way it did."

"What does that mean?"

"I went over to Lakeshore Manor that day, and when I accidentally knocked that bike over, I thought I saw someone on the second floor. So I was sure someone—at least Sou—was inside the house, so I rang the doorbell, but no one came to the door. And so I went around to the back door.

"That door was open, and when I went inside, I saw someone's shoes. A pair of dirty sneakers smaller than mine..."

Mei had gone up to the second floor. She'd had the impression that she'd seen a person in the window of the library, so she'd headed straight there and—

"At exactly that second, the owl clock on the opposite wall rang and distracted me. And while my attention was focused on one of Kirika's dolls on a display shelf, I walked into the room..."

At that point, Sou was standing in front of the desk by the left wall, which was in Mei's blind spot since she could only see out of her right eye—

"It was really as simple as **I couldn't physically see him**." Mei pointed at her eye patch. "But right after that—"

"You took your eye patch off."

"It was dirty and felt gross, so I took it off. Almost at the same second, a bunch of crows flew past the window…"

Crows? Oh right—maybe I did remember her saying that.

"It surprised me, and I looked over at the window. Even though it was cloudy that day, the window was bright and it was dim inside the room, but since the crows were going past the window, it made it darker outside. In that moment, the intensity of light and dark flipped and the inside of the room was reflected on the window glass. That's how—"

"Ah…I see."

The situation drew itself as a picture in my mind, and finally I realized and could understand.

Mei said, "I saw the outline of Sou standing right there. Obviously in my right eye, not my left. It surprised me, and when I spun around to look at him, he was standing in front of the desk, so I…"

"*Why?*"

Mei had whispered reflexively.

"*Why…are you in a place like that?*"

"**Can you really see me?**" Sou had asked, startled and caught off guard.

"*Yes…I can…,*" Mei had replied frankly.

"When Sou and I talked after that, we were out of step with each other at first, but he was so serious about it when he told me, 'Mr. Sakaki is dead' and 'I'm his ghost'…In the end, I got into the habit of following his lead. I asked him about the details of what had happened up to that point…and while I was listening, I started to understand what was going on in Sou's mind. Once I did, somehow I understood that pointing out to him 'but you're Sou' right then and there would have been bad..."

"And then two days later you decided to look into it. You asked Kirika to invite the Hiratsuka family over to your house."

"That's right."

Mei ran the middle finger of her left hand down across her eye patch.

"I wanted to find out, first of all, what had actually happened to Mr. Sakaki. In other words, how much of Sou's story was true. I wanted to see how he acted when he was with Tsukiho and his family..."

Instead of nodding, I let out a long sigh.

I thought I was used to this by now, but I was starting to feel myself being swallowed up in the atmosphere of this basement room so dominated by the "emptiness" of the dolls. And so somehow, despite our discussion of the "underlying truth," I was starting to feel as if **we were the ones** who were really the "mirage"...

Maybe she guessed what was happening—

"You want to go somewhere else?" Mei suggested. "Let's go to the sofas upstairs. We're mostly done with the story anyway."

6

Thinking about it, I was pretty sure this was the first time I had been in the first-floor gallery without Grandma Amane being there. The gallery was closed, so the string music that always played was also missing. The air-conditioning wasn't on, either, and it felt a little muggy compared to the basement—

When we sat down on the sofas that faced each other at an angle, I felt as if I could hear, unpleasantly clearly, Mei's breathing and all its subtle changes…And even at this late point, I felt a little fidgety. My heart was racing.

Mei had brought her sketchbook upstairs with her and started to set it down on the armrest of the sofa, but before she did, she murmured to herself, "Oh right," and instead placed the sketchbook on her lap. I wondered what that had been about but pressed ahead.

"So hey, that reminds me.

"What was going on with that friend Arai who called Mr. Sakaki? Did you not ever figure it out?"

"No."

As Mei shook her head very slightly, she opened the sketchbook. But the picture of Lakeshore Manor she'd drawn last summer…was not what she now showed me.

She opened the sketchbook up to just before the back cover. I could see a light blue envelope slipped between two pages.

"I tried to check that," Mei said offhandedly. "It bothered me, too, so that night—while I was looking for Sou, I got the idea to try calling."

"Oh?"

"Because the message and caller's phone number were both still on the base set of the phone in the hall. So I tried calling that number. I asked, 'Is this Arai's house?' "

Ah. No deep thought required—that was the fastest way to check certainly.

"—And?"

"A really old man came onto the phone. It wasn't him, but when I asked if it was Arai's house, he told me it wasn't. So I changed my question and asked, 'Okay, is Arai there?' and he said, 'There's no one here by that name,' in a really harsh way."

I was just wondering what that could mean, when Mei picked up the envelope that had been stuck into her sketchbook and pulled something out of it.

"Here, look at this."

She held out a photograph. When I looked at it, a small noise escaped me. "Oh…Is this it?"

"Mr. Sakaki's 'photo that brings back so many memories' from summer vacation eleven years ago."

"This is…"

I studied the photo intently.

The date the picture was taken, "8/3/1987," was indeed printed in the lower right of the image.

A mixed group of five girls and boys lined up with a lake behind them. So the boy on the far right was Teruya Sakaki. He was a different age than in the photo Mei had first shown me from last year, but it was definitely the same person. The other four had been students in third-year Class 3 at North Yomi…

"And the notes are here."

She next held out the notepaper, which I took to read the figures' names.

In order from the right, they were "Sakaki," "Yagisawa," "Higuchi," "Mitarai," and "Arai."

Just like Mei had said in her story, below "Yagisawa" and "Arai" was written an "X" and the word "dead."

"I tried to play it innocent on the phone. I said, 'I'm sorry, whose house is this, then?' And then the answer was—"

Mei cast her eyes down to the photo I held in my hands.

"They said, 'This is the Mitarai house.'"

"Mitarai?"

"The second from the left in the picture. The chubby kid with the glasses and blue T-shirt. Apparently it was his house. Mitarai."

"But the message on the answering machine was from Arai…," I started to protest, then realized: "But maybe Arai was something else."

"It could have been Mitarai's nickname or what his friends called him. Just taking the last part of his name and calling him Arai instead."

"But what about this person with the 'X'?"

"If that person's name were Arai, too, it would be confusing, right? So I think it's a different reading of the characters. Like *Nii* instead of *Arai*."

"—Oh yeah."

"It was Nii who died all those years ago. Mitarai is alive and had been keeping in touch with Mr. Sakaki. He just happened to call him up…Probably he needed something, like he was going to ask him to lend him some money or something."

Looking at it this way, the truth was almost humorous. For the "ghost of Sakaki" (i.e., Sou), who lacked the knowledge that Arai was Mitarai, it definitely would have been shocking and confused him.

—But even so.

What was this photo doing here? Had Mei taken it from the library in Lakeshore Manor? Or maybe…

I glanced at Mei's hands.

The light blue envelope, just big enough to hold a photograph. I spotted something written on the face of the envelope and a stamp.

Had someone mailed it to her? If so, who?

Before I could ask, Mei said, "By the way…Sakakibara.

"When you look at that photo, do you sense anything?"

7

"Like what?"

My eyes fell once again to the photograph from eleven years ago.

The students of the 1987 third-year Class 3 at Yomiyama North Middle. Who had been invited by Teruya Sakaki to share a peaceful moment over summer break at Lakeshore Manor in Hinami, unaffected by the "disasters." But afterward, of the four who had returned to Yomiyama, Yagisawa and Nii had lost their lives…

"…I'm not sure."

I looked into Mei's face. At that, her right eye narrowed slyly.

"You don't feel like **the spacing is unnatural?**"

"Huh?"

I looked back at the photo.

An unnatural space? An unnatural…

"…Oh!"

Here?

Teruya Sakaki on the far right and to his left the girl called Yagisawa. Here, between the two of them…

"They're standing apart from each other. Mr. Sakaki and Yagisawa," Mei said. "Don't you think it's weird how far apart they are from each other? Almost like…"

"Yeah. It's almost like…"

As I was responding, I was remembering something. The two photos we had taken in front of the gate to Sakitani Memorial Hall on the class trip in August.

Both showed five people.

The first one was me, Mei, Kazami, Teshigawara, and Ms. Mikami in that order. In the second one, Teshigawara had been replaced by Mochizuki, who was pressed right up against "his beloved Ms. Mikami"…

…*Vmm…vmmmmm…*

A low-frequency noise started up somewhere in my head.

If I were to look at those photos five or ten years from now, how would they appear to me? That was the question. As time passed, my memories of the "extra person"/"the casualty" from this year would fade and disappear…*Vmm…vmmmmm…*and **she** would vanish from the photos. And then **an unnatural space where a**

picture of someone had originally been but no longer appeared would develop in her place…

"…This is…," I said, my eyes still fixed on the photo in my hand. Without realizing it, my empty hand had been pressed over my chest. My voice was panting and short of breath. "Could it be that originally there was—that this picture used to show **someone** beside Mr. Sakaki?"

"You get that feeling, right?"

"Y…yeah."

"That's what I think. **Someone** used to be in this picture. That it must have been 'the casualty' who'd infiltrated third-year Class 3 eleven years ago. And—"

Mei cut herself off suggestively and ran her slender fingers down the white of her eye patch. She seemed to be saying, "You know what I'm going to say next," but I had no idea at all.

"And well," Mei continued. "I was thinking maybe that **someone** was Mr. Sakaki's first love."

"Wha—?"

"Because apparently, in all the different conversations he had with Sou, Mr. Sakaki said something like this…"

†   †

So, have you? Ever been in love? Who was your first love?

……

You didn't have one?

No…I suppose I did.

What does it feel like to be in love? Is it fun? Does it hurt?

It's…Oh, I don't know. I'm not sure I'm qualified to answer these questions.

Why not?

…Because I can't remember.

†

Caring so much…Yeah, that's definitely true. I remember that. I think I cared…a lot. But…

But what?

I just can't remember. No matter how hard I try, I can't remember who that person was.

†   †

"I told you how there was an 'archive of the disasters' on the second floor of Lakeshore Manor, right? These words were written on the wall of that room: 'Who are you? Who were you?'"

"Yeah…you did."

"At the point this photo was taken, during summer break, of course Mr. Sakaki didn't know who the casualty was for that year, and neither did anyone else. There's no way they could have known. So maybe during that time, Mr. Sakaki started to like **her**. Never knowing that she was the casualty…"

After the graduation ceremony in 1987, when the phenomenon for that year ended and the casualty disappeared, all the various records that had been altered to make things consistent would return to normal. It would turn out that she had never existed **in that year**, and eventually she would disappear from the memories of the people involved and over a long enough time, **she** would vanish.

Even the memories of Teruya Sakaki, who had loved **her**, could not escape this rule.

Maybe Sakaki had even found out that **she** had been that year's casualty from his North Yomi classmate Mitarai after the graduation ceremony. His memories of being in love with **her**, of liking her so much—that impression on his heart had lasted inside him even after **she** had disappeared. But the girl's name, face, voice, the words they had spoken to each other, the time they had spent together...all those memories had inevitably faded as time went on and disappeared. And then after however many years, he was no longer able to remember all the things he had shared with **her**. That's why—

That's why he...

8

"That might be the biggest reason Mr. Sakaki was entranced by death."

After a few seconds of silence, I spoke the thought as it occurred to me.

"If he died, he could connect with everyone who had died before. But maybe it was **her** he wanted to connect with more than 'everyone.'"

"—Could be," Mei responded, her gaze cast downward. "Although...that's a feeling I don't really understand."

"Really...?"

"I don't think I've ever cared about someone that much."

"You don't think?"

"Yeah. I'm not sure."

Letting out a quiet sigh, I took another look at the photo that brought back so many memories of eleven years ago.

The unnatural space between Teruya Sakaki and Whoever Yagisawa. No—no matter how hard I squinted, I couldn't see anybody there.

A fifteen-year-old Teruya Sakaki holding a brown cane in his left hand and resting his right hand on his hip, smiling. The sheer happiness in his smile left me feeling incredibly sad.

"Have you figured out the last puzzle left?" Mei's voice broke in on my thoughts.

"What puzzle?" I lifted my eyes from the photo.

"Of Mr. Sakaki's last words."

"Oh...that 'tsu' and 'ki' stuff?"

"Yeah."

"Well..."

I had been thinking he really was saying the "tsuki" in Tsukiho.

Like maybe he wanted to say something to her at the very, very end, since she had tried to stop him from committing suicide. Or maybe—

"We can drill even deeper into it. Look at it as the 'dying message' someone speaks in a mystery novel."

"Oh yeah?" Mei narrowed her right eye dubiously. I outlined my thought.

"Say Tsukiho had actually pushed Mr. Sakaki over the railing deliberately. When Mr. Sakaki finally fell from the second-floor corridor, he picked up on the murderous intent directed at him, and..."

"He wanted to tell someone that Tsukiho was the culprit?"

"Well, from his perspective anyway."

At that, Mei pursed her lips a little and looked at me, almost scowling.

"Overruled," she said. "If that were the case, wouldn't the expression on Mr. Sakaki's face right before he died, which Sou saw, be strange? He said his expression was oddly peaceful...as if he'd been freed from suffering, and fear, and anxiety. Because 'tsu...ki' is what he said in that moment."

"Hmmm. When you put it that way, you're right. So then..."

So then what could it have been? I cocked my head in thought.

What had he been saying at the very end…?

"I stopped by the secondary library recently, actually. To see Mr. Chibiki," Mei said. I was caught a little flat-footed.

"Why'd you go back?"

"I wanted to see that file."

What file?…The one Mr. Chibiki kept? That folder with the pitch-black cover where he kept copies of the class lists for the last twenty-seven years, from the year it started twenty-six years ago up to this year?

"For whatever reason, while all kinds of records are compromised by the 'phenomenon' and go back to normal, that file is apparently the only thing that is partially **overlooked**. Notes on the name of the casualty for an on year especially. So I wanted to check it and see."

When she said that, I was finally able to guess.

"To see who was the casualty in 1987?"

"Mr. Sakaki didn't know about this, remember. If he had, he might have been able to go and check it himself."

Since he had changed schools early on, he probably hadn't had a chance to come into contact with Mr. Chibiki. So he wouldn't have had any way of learning that the file existed—

"And I found out her name. The casualty in 1987."

"The girl who was Mr. Sakaki's first love?"

Mei nodded silently.

"It was Satsuki."

She spoke her name.

"Satsuki Shinomiya."

With "Shinomiya" written with the characters for *four halls* and "Satsuki" written with characters that could read *hope on a sandy shore*.

"See? So…"

So…of course.

"You mean 'tsu…ki' was him saying 'Satsuki'?"

"Staring death in the face, maybe Mr. Sakaki remembered. That **her** name was Satsuki. And that's why his expression was so peaceful..."

He hadn't spoken the "sa" aloud and had barely managed the "tsu" and "ki." So the round shape of his mouth afterward—what had looked like the vowel O—had simply been him trying to breathe out in relief. Or perhaps after saying her name, he had started to say something like "You..."

"That's just me conjecturing, though," Mei added, and she let out a short sigh.

9

Sakaki and Satsuki, eleven years ago...

Looking at the photo I held, my mind turned over the coincidence.

Satsuki could be written with the characters for *fifth month*. In other words, May. Like Mei...

Oh, whatever, it's not even anything...

...Vmm...vmmmmm...

Wanting to shake off the faint, low frequency that had once again started up, I sluggishly shook my head.

"This came yesterday," Mei said just then. A light blue envelope had been tucked into her sketchbook. She had now laid the envelope on the table and was pointing at it.

"From who?" I asked. "Who sent you that?"

"Sou," Mei replied. Then, she picked the envelope up again. "He sent me that photo and the note and also this letter."

She pulled out a letter, folded in half, on paper the same color as the envelope and held it out to me.

"Is it okay if I read it, too?"

"Sure."

This is what was written in the letter. In an extremely skilled adult hand—

I am doing well now.

I hope you will accept this photograph.

If you do not want it, please feel free to throw it out.

I, too, will be in middle school next spring.

I hope to see you again sometime.

Without a word, I handed the photo, note, and letter all back to Mei. She put them back into the envelope; then, though she said nothing, she turned the envelope facedown and rested it on top of her sketchbook—

That was when the name and address of the sender, written on the back of the envelope, came to my attention. I didn't grasp the meaning of it all at once. "No—" I heard myself say, and turned to ask Mei, "How...When?"

"I don't know the details...but he didn't want to stay with his family in Hinami anymore."

"But this address—"

"Maybe it's a relative or someone he knows. They've taken him into their house for the time being."

"Oh...but..."

For a short time, I was unable to tear my eyes from the letters that marched across the envelope. I was totally incapable of calming the spread of an unsettling apprehension, but I had the strong impression that it would be wrong to voice it here.

I felt a faint breeze then, even though the air conditioner was off.

The air rustled chill.
The address read: "Akazawa home, 6-6 Tobii District, Yomiyama."
And below that, the name—
Not "Sou Hiratsuka," but simply "Sou."

The End

Afterword

While writing, I had imagined *Another* as a long-form one-off.

At the very least, I had thought that the story of Koichi Sakaki-bara and Mei Misaki against the backdrop of Yomiyama in the year 1998 would end there—but then the magazine serialization ended and the story was put out in paperback. Out of nowhere, I watched a multimedia empire develop around it, and my thinking started to change. *I wouldn't mind writing a little more about Mei Misaki, still at age fifteen in 1998,* I thought.

At that point, my mind hit on the "blank space of over a week" when Mei left Yomiyama and went with her family to their sea-side vacation home, before the class trip over the summer. I could tell a story where she actually got involved in **some sort of incident** during that time that Koichi doesn't know about…

Playing with various ideas along these lines, I started to see what I was going to do.

The title was the first thing I decided on: *Another Episode S.*

The *S* of *Episode S* is for "summer," for "seaside," for "secret," for the character who becomes the narrator, "the other person named Sakaki"…I could go even further and mention the *S* of "shitai" (corpse) and "shinkirou" (mirage), too.

Still, this started out positioned as a side story or a spin-off of *Another*, but I started to feel like it couldn't really be a spin-off when Mei Misaki is the heroine. Not only that, but the present day where Mei is telling Koichi the details of the incident is after the final scene of the original *Another* books—at the end of September 1998. From a timeline perspective, I came to believe it might not be entirely unreasonable to call this a sequel.

This novel has rather a different flavor from the original *Another*, though it keeps the aforementioned troubling phenomenon that occurs in third-year Class 3 at Yomiyama North Middle as a shared dominant note. It might have something of a perplexing bent, but now that the story is complete, I can't help but feel it might have been necessary to position a story like this here. And once it was done, it also struck me that, in some sense, it turned out to be quite an Ayatsuji-esque novel.

I hope you'll enjoy it.

I have a few other ideas (delusions?) for sequels to *Another*.

I can't know for sure which of these will ever be written, but presumably much depends on the desires of you, the readers. The rest is just a question of my mental and physical resources. In any event, I'm going to take a little while to recharge and let the fantasies run wild.

During my run through ten total issues in the *Syousetsuya Sari-sari* magazine, my editor Ms. Akiko Kanako was always an incredible help. I give her my gratitude for every last bit of it. Thanks also go to Mr. Shinichiro Inoue, who gave me many insightful suggestions during the idea phase. I would also like to take this opportunity to thank the cover artist Ms. Shiho Toda and the formatter Ms. Kumi Suzuki, as well as Ms. Akiko Fukazawa, Ms. Kaori Ichiji, Mr. Ryo Nakamura, and all the people at Kadokawa Shoten who were such a great help to me.

Early Summer 2013
Yukito Ayatsuji

The pages of
the manga have
been presented
in their original
right-to-left
reading order.

The story begins
at the back
of the book,
on page 282.

The story begins
at the back
of the book,
on page 282.

Another0

Another 0

Afterword

Since I had never worked on anything more than stand-alone books before, getting to spend a little over two years and four total books on a story like *Another* has been truly special for me.

This piece collects an *Another* side story. I begged Ayatsuji-sensei to let me write a story for Reiko-san, and he graciously agreed. I hope you enjoyed it.

—Hiro Kiyohara

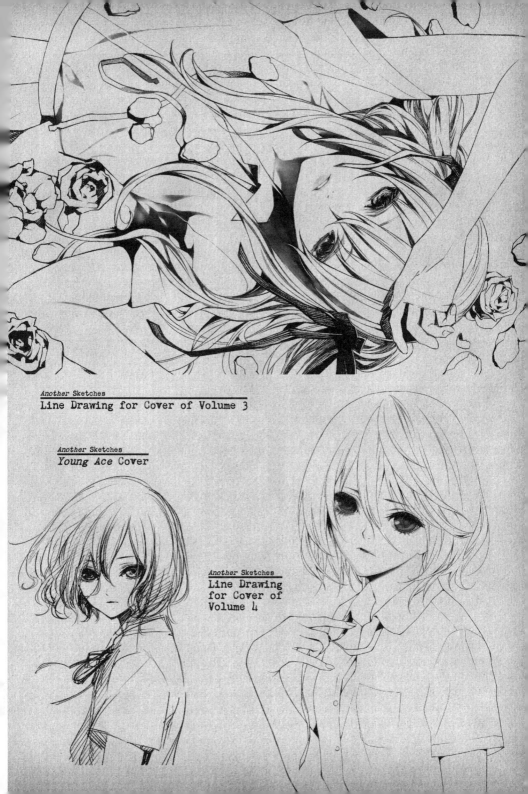

Another Sketches
Line Drawing for Cover of Volume 3

Another Sketches
Young Ace Cover

Another Sketches
Line Drawing
for Cover of
Volume 4

(B)

Another Sketches
Line Drawing for Cover of
Volume 1

26 years ago

White hair

Gentle-
manly
beard?

Chibiki-
sensei

- Slender, tall
- Clothes are all black
- Middle-aged?
- Black-framed glasses

Another Sketches
Yukari Sakuragi Sketch

Name Tag

桜木

Sakuragi

Plastic laminated
onto a card, pinned
to the uniform

- Class representative
- Silver-rimmed glasses
- She's supposed to be
plump, but I changed
her to skinny.

Check
pattern
could work,
too...

Bleached brown

- Comes off ditzy
- Flashy, but trendy

- Comes off ditzy
- Flashy, but trendy

One fold

- Glasses
- Thin, elegant face

Another Sketches
Reiko Mikami
Sketch

Easy-going

Wears sweats at home

Heh-heh...

Reiko!

Late 20s (29?)

*Black hair

- Looks casual at home
  (sweater or baggy clothes)
- Apron & T-shirt in her studio
- Glasses on at school
- Hair tied back and looks
  put-together

Looks
a bit
mature

Eyes mostly
languorous

Ears slightly
covered

Summer

Winter

Petite girl
with short,
shaggy bob

Height: 148 cm

Mussed bob haircut

Super-deformed

...

Another 0

sketches

Hiro Kiyohara

Another Sketches
Line Art of Opening Image

Another0

OH...

I'M GOING TO BE STAYING HERE STARTING TODAY.

HOPE I DON'T BOTHER YOU TOO MUCH.

BACK THEN...

...THERE WAS NOTHING I COULD DO.

BUT NOW... THERE IS.

EVEN IF THE DISASTERS START UP THIS YEAR...

—*I WILL PROTECT KOICHI-KUN.*

SO DON'T WORRY...

...NEE-SAN.

COME ON IN, NOW, KOICHI-CHAN.

REIKOOOO? WE'RE HOME!

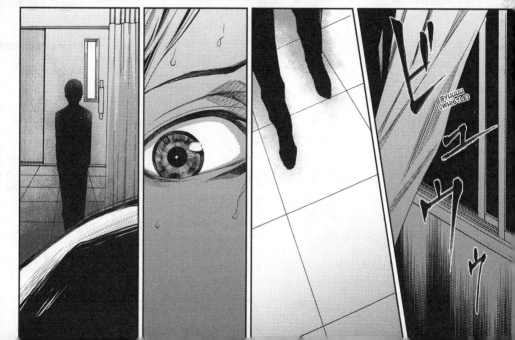

...OKAY.

GUH
...

IT...

I THINK IT'S VERY UNBECOMING TO GIVE UP BEFORE YOU EVEN TRY.

NO MATTER WHERE YOU DECIDE YOUR FUTURE IS...

...IF YOU REALLY WANT TO GO FOR IT, THERE'S NO REASON TO BE AFRAID.

SO HAVE SOME MORE CONFIDENCE IN YOURSELF.

AND IF IT TURNS OUT AWFUL EVEN WHEN YOU TRY YOUR BEST...

WHETHER YOU'RE COOL OR NOT.

OH, IT'S SUPER-IMPORTANT THOUGH.

...WHO CARES.

...YOUR BIG SISTER WILL LOOK OUT FOR YOU.

IT'S ALL
RIGHT.

IT'S ALL
RIGHT. I'M
HERE FOR
YOU.

I DON'T
KNOW WHAT
YOU'RE
STRUGGLING
WITH INSIDE...

...BUT
IT'S ALL
RIGHT.

NO MATTER
WHAT HAPPENS,
I'LL BE THERE
FOR YOU.

EVERYONE IN CLASS LOOKS NERVOUS.

IF THIS KEEPS GOING, WHO KNOWS WHEN THE NEXT VICTIM WILL...

SENSEI ...!

I DON'T KNOW...

THE ONLY THING I CAN DO IS SERVE AS AN OBSERVER TO GATHER INFORMATION...

I'M SORRY THIS DIDN'T TURN OUT AS YOU HOPED.

AFTER THIS PHENOM-ENON BEGAN...

...I'VE TRIED VARIOUS STRATEGIES... EVEN AFTER I FLED INTO THIS ROLE AS LIBRARIAN...

...BUT THE RESULT WAS ALWAYS THE SAME... A GREAT NUMBER OF PEOPLE DIED.

I SEE... AND THERE'S THAT RULE THAT YOU CAN'T TALK TO YOUR *FAMILY* ABOUT IT.

SO WHAT IS IT YOU'D LIKE TO ASK ME, THEN?

...I WANT TO KNOW HOW TO STOP THE DISASTERS.

AH, I SEE. SO YOU'RE RITSUKO'S LITTLE SISTER.

DID YOUR SISTER TELL YOU ABOUT ME?

AFTER WHAT HAPPENED, I COULDN'T STOP THINKING ABOUT IT. SO I LOOKED THROUGH A YEARBOOK FROM THE YEAR IT HAPPENED.

IT SAID YOU WERE THE HEAD TEACHER FOR THIRD-YEAR CLASS 3...

UM... HERE...

I FOUND THIS IN MY SISTER'S ROOM...IT'S A GROUP PHOTO WITH MISAKI IN IT.

THIS IS...

!

KO
(TAK)

THIS IS NO GOOD...

I CAN'T CONCENTRATE AT ALL...

SCHOOL LET OUT LONG AGO.

I'M CLOSING UP HERE, SO YOU NEED TO GO HOME.

OH! I'M SORR—

I MEAN... COULD I TALK TO YOU FOR A SECOND?

UM, EXCUSE ME!

YOU'RE... CHIBIKI-SENSEI, RIGHT?

AHH... SHE'S A BIT...

WELL, YOU KNOW, HER FRIEND JUST DIED, AFTER ALL.

I FEEL LIKE REIKO HASN'T COME BY LATELY...

HEY, MOM?

....

OH.

PAKI (SNAP)

ARGH!

NO WAY... LAST WEEK IT WAS AKIYAMA-SAN. NOW TWO PEOPLE HAVE...

BUT IF THAT'S TRUE, THEN...

HEY.

COULD THIS BE...

IT'S JUST A COINCIDENCE, ISN'T IT?

...YEAH.

IT'S THE DISASTERS.

WHEN THAT HAPPENS...

...EVERY MONTH, AT LEAST ONE PERSON LINKED TO THE CLASS WILL LOSE THEIR LIFE...

...IS IT REAL?

I'VE JUST... RECEIVED WORD...

...THAT...

BUT—

...KURIDA-KUN, WHO HAS BEEN ABSENT...

HIS HEALTH DETERIORATED AND HE APPARENTLY PASSED AWAY THIS MORNING.

RYOKO AKIYAMA.

MY FRIEND. WE WERE CLOSE, EVER SINCE FIRST YEAR.

SHE WAS IN A TRAFFIC ACCIDENT ON HER WAY HOME FROM SCHOOL, AND SHE DIED.

HER DEATH MADE ME SO SAD...

...I COULDN'T THINK ABOUT ANYTHING ELSE.

Another 0

IT CAN'T BE...

APPARENTLY... PEOPLE REALLY DO DIE IN DISASTERS DURING AN "ON YEAR."

AND A LOT OF THEM, AT THAT—...

THE DISASTERS ARE REAL.

—YOU SHOULD BE CARE-FUL.

AnotherØ

Part 1
End

THERE WAS AN ACCIDENT ON THE WAY HOME FROM SCHOOL, AND A GIRL PASSED AWAY...
THAT GIRL YOU'VE BEEN FRIENDS WITH SINCE FIRST YEAR... AKIYAMA-SAN.

NO WAY THERE'S A "CURSE."

REIKO, YOU'RE NOT GOING HOME YET?

NOPE. I'VE GOT CLUB TODAY.

I'LL SEE YOU TOMORROW, THEN.

BYUO (WLIGOH)

I'M GONNA FINISH THIS ONE TODAY.

BACK THEN...

...I STILL BELIEVED THAT.

...WHAT?

GEEZ, WHAT ARE YOU DOING?

CLASS IS ABOUT TO START!

HE'S TOTALLY UNFRIENDLY AND ALWAYS DRESSES IN ALL BLACK.

HE'S HARD TO TALK TO.

HUH...

THAT'S CHIBIKI-SENSEI.

I'M PRETTY SURE HE'S A LIBRARIAN.

DO YOU KNOW WHO THAT MAN IS...?

YEAH.

APPARENTLY... PEOPLE REALLY DO DIE IN DISASTERS DURING AN "ON YEAR."

AND A LOT OF THEM, AT THAT—...

YOU KNOW STUFF LIKE THAT CREEPS ME OUT.

C... CUT IT OUT.

LIKE THAT LADY WITH CUT-OPEN CHEEKS THAT EVERYONE WAS TALKING ABOUT A LITTLE WHILE BACK— THAT WAS AWESOME.

HEY, SORRY.

I'M INTO THIS STUFF, SO...

....

THEY SAY THE DISASTERS AFFECT MEMBERS OF THE CLASS AND THEIR FAMILIES OUT TO TWO DEGREES.

ALSO, THE FARTHER AWAY FROM THIS TOWN YOU GO, THE WEAKER THE EFFECT BECOMES.

LET'S SEE...

OH, THERE IT IS!

OH...

I JUST REMEMBERED, THERE'S A BOOK I WANTED TO BORROW.

HOLD ON A SECOND.

MY SISTER'S ALWAYS BEEN ON MY SIDE.

AND—

I'VE ALWAYS LOOKED UP TO HER.

THE FACTS BEHIND THE CURSE?

YUP.

I ASKED SOME OF THE PREVIOUS STUDENTS ABOUT IT, DID SOME RESEARCH...

...AND FOUND OUT SOMETHING INTERESTING.

OOH, OKAY. I GET IT, I GET IT.

DAD WAS JUST SO—

URGGGGH!

YOU HAD ANOTHER FIGHT WITH DAD ABOUT YOUR FUTURE?

I HEARD YOU KNOW

THAT WAS...

MY MUCH OLDER SISTER RITSUKO.

SHE'S MARRIED AND LIVES IN TOKYO NOW.

BUT RIGHT NOW SHE'S BACK HOME IN YOMIYAMA TO HAVE HER BABY.

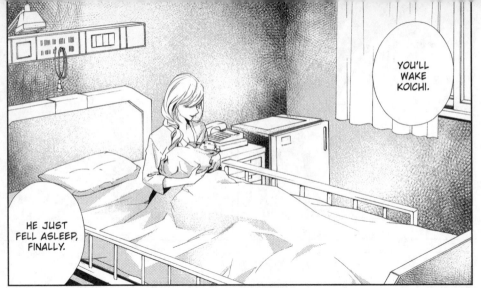

YOU'LL WAKE KOICHI.

HE JUST FELL ASLEEP, FINALLY.

THERE, THERE.

ANYWAY, ARE YOU SURE YOU HAVE TIME TO BE VISITING EVERY DAY?

YOU'RE A THIRD-YEAR NOW, YOU NEED TO THINK ABOUT EXAMS...

URK...!

DON'T BE SILLY.

HE'S SOOOOOO CUUUUUTE.

OHHH, I WISH HE WERE MINE!!

....

NO WAY.

SHH!

ONEE-CHAN!

GARA
(CLATTER)

HUFF!

HUFF
...!

WHEN THE SEMESTER STARTS IN AN "ON YEAR," THEY WIND UP BEING SHORT ONE DESK AND CHAIR.

A LONG TIME AGO, A STUDENT NAMED MISAKI DIED, AND EVER SINCE—

AND APPARENTLY THIS YEAR IS AN "ON YEAR."

THEY WERE ONE SHORT...

WHEN THAT HAPPENS...

AND SO.

....

...EVERY MONTH, AT LEAST ONE PERSON LINKED TO THE CLASS...

...WILL LOSE THEIR LIFE IN SOME KIND OF AN ACCIDENT OR AN ILLNESS...

I... I'M TALLER NOW, FOR ONE...

WELL, YOU'VE STILL GOT THE CHEST OF A LITTLE KID.

AND I CAN TAKE THE TRAIN BY MYSELF NOW...

WE'RE IN THIRD YEAR NOW! BUT YOU HAVEN'T CHANGED AT ALL...

YOU NEED TO GET WITH THE PROGRAM.

I BET YOU WERE UP ALL NIGHT DRAWING AGAIN!

DON'T GIVE ME THAT!

NAME ONE THING.

COME ON, IT'S NOT THAT BAD.

I'VE GROWN UP A LOT!

SOMEDAY I'M...

—NEVER MIND THAT...DID YOU HEAR?

...GONNA BE LIKE MY BIG SISTER...

THE RUMORS ABOUT THIRD-YEAR CLASS 3?

THE STORY OF THE "CURSED THIRD-YEAR CLASS 3"?

GAYA

GAYA (CHATTER)

REIKO.

MORNING.

ACK!

三年三組

SIGN: THIRD YEAR CLASS 3

OH...

M—

MORNING.

RITSUKO-
NEESAN...

FIFTEEN
YEARS
AGO

APRIL
1983

I WAS A
THIRD-YEAR
IN MIDDLE
SCHOOL.

—NEE-SAN.

DID YOU KNOW?

WE'RE LOOKING AFTER KOICHI-KUN NOW.

JUST FOR HIS THIRD YEAR OF MIDDLE SCHOOL, ANYWAY.

IT'S BEEN MORE THAN FIFTEEN YEARS SINCE YOU DIED, SIS.

I'M TOTALLY OVER THE HILL NOW.

I... I WONDER IF I'VE GROWN UP AT ALL SINCE THEN?

WHAT DO YOU THINK?

Part 1